THE WINTER HEALS

THE WINTER HEALS

MARIE MCGRATH

ALSO BY MARIE MCGRATH

Other works by Marie McGrath

Novels

The Many Faces of Charlotte Barnes

The Fall Changes

Anthologies

Christmas Magic

Coming Soon!

The Spring Renews- Coming May 2021

For the latest news and updates, please check out Marie McGrath on her social media pages. Exclusive content and sneak peeks can be found in her FB Fan Page.

Twitter: @Marie_McGrath_

Instagram: marie_mcgrath_

Facebook: www.facebook.com/MarieMcGrathAuthor

Facebook Fan Page: www.facebook.com/groups/MarieMcGrathFans

Website:

https://mariemcgrathauthor.wixsite.com/books

ISBN: paperback 978-1-7332621-9-4

Any references to historical events, real people or real places are used
fictitiously. Names, characters, and places are products of the author's
imagination.
Cover Design by Diana TC, triumphcovers.com
Edited by Brian Paone
Logo by Kevin Harless
First Printing Edition 2021
Published by Creative James Media
Pasadena, MD 21122

❀ Created with Vellum

To all those who just want to heal, but someone stops them

CHAPTER 1

I stared at my name in the perfectly done calligraphy. The place cards for my mother's event had to be done precisely. It looked so pretentious. *How fitting.* Mother was all about the pomp and circumstance. I used to love it as well, but lately, I just didn't care about it anymore.

"What do you think? Isn't it just perfect?" Mother asked.

"It's something, Mother."

"Now, Shelby, what's the matter with you?"

My chest tightened. "Nothing. It's perfect." It *was* perfect, but it just wasn't for me anymore. How did I fight something instilled since birth? Was that even possible?

Mother always said, *"You're a Rowe, Shelby. Rowes are like royalty here in Honey Cove. You need to remember that others are looking up to us, and you are part of that. You need to act like the queen, because one day, you'll be the queen of this family and the honorary queen of the town."*

I didn't want any of it. Sure, I liked being noticed and having things, but that's all they were, just *things*.

"Of course, it is. Only a few more days and our annual Christmas ball will have its fifteenth year! I never could have imagined it would get so extravagant." She stopped and faced me. "You know, someday this will all be yours. You'll choose the place settings, the name cards, the decorations. Everything. Doesn't that sound wonderful?"

I nodded more from necessity than true desire. My mother would never understand my change. Even I didn't understand what had happened. This school year changed everything. The things I enjoyed no longer had the same luster.

"Well, you better get ready for school. Today is your last day before Christmas break, right?"

"Yes. I'll see you after school."

Mother waved and refocused on the name cards.

I was sure she would agonize over those names all day, making changes over and over and ultimately settling for this exact font anyway. To be Vivian Rowe meant appearances were important, and events had to be perfect. As her daughter, I had a similar role I was burdened to carry.

I ascended the front grand staircase, exiting the large ballroom, which was home to the Christmas ball. Once in my bedroom, I headed for my massive walk-in closet. My mood wasn't ready for the outfit Tabitha and Priscilla had expected me to wear today. We were supposed to match, but I didn't want to. My social position had exhausted me, and wearing a matching outfit seemed to be too much to cope with at the moment.

I sighed dejectedly and settled on my favorite pair of jeans with a gray turtleneck and brown ankle boots. The color of the turtleneck would complement my pale blue eyes. Completely dressed, I slugged my bookbag over my shoulder and trudged downstairs.

The foyer was vacant of staff and my mother. Was it too much to expect her to say goodbye before I went to school?

No doubt she was still in the massive hall, figuring out all the details for her precious ball.

I'm only important when it suits her.

I needed to pull it together. Giving into self-pity and loathing wouldn't help an already tiresome day. The sooner I arrived at school, the sooner the day would be over, then I could focus on more important things during break.

~

"We were supposed to wear our matching velvet dresses with white puffed sleeves today, Shelby!" Priscilla trilled.

I shrugged. "Wasn't feeling it." My books laid crammed in my locker, the noise drowning out both of them as I added each new one.

"What's with you, Shelby?" Tabitha asked.

"You're different, and I don't like it," Priscilla said.

"I'm different? Are you sure about that?"

Tabitha shifted her gaze between us. "You never pass up matching outfits."

"Well, maybe I'm not interested in matching with you after you two acted devious, blamed me for it, and then expected us to be fine." I scoffed. "I'm not the one who's different."

Priscilla scowled. "That remark is proof. You would have *helped* us before."

Tabitha huffed. "You know how many girls we've made fun of? Especially ones from backgrounds like her?"

"Now you're making excuses for *her*," Priscilla said.

"*Her* name is Riley, and what you two did on that app was horrendous. Whatever I may have done before, I didn't condone that and still don't."

"That was over two months ago. Are you still going on about that?"

I slammed my locker door. "Yes. Now, if you'll excuse me, I have class to attend."

Priscilla and Tabitha crossed their arms and snarled. They were downright awful lately.

How had I ever been friends with them? I cringed. What was worse was they were right. I used to partake in the same behavior. It had been the three of us since we were little. Our families were connected, and it was expected that we would be best friends. It didn't help we were all founding families. Our social circles would be connected for life.

I frowned. How had things become so complicated lately? It was easier before Riley Mills came to Honey Cove. Since the first day, I felt different, and I couldn't explain it. Maybe it was time for a change, and Riley sparked it? I shook my head. Whatever it was, I must sort it out, or life would get more complicated. Priscilla and Tabitha wouldn't go away easily, especially because of the social standing they benefited from being near me. We all benefited from our ancestry in this small town, yet it didn't feel right anymore.

I stood in front of my science classroom. All my thoughts and questions bombarded me from moving forward.

"It's nice of you to join us, Ms. Rowe," Mr. Boone said. "Do you plan to attend my science class today or stand in the hallway?"

I peered around Mr. Boone into the room. A few of the cheerleaders sitting at the front giggled.

"Of course, Mr. Boone," I said and sat in my usual seat.

The cheerleaders spun around and watched me then spoke in hushed tones. I didn't have to guess to know they were discussing me.

What was I doing? My classmates revered me out of fear. If people got word of my soft spot, I would be ruined. I didn't need that in high school, nor did I need my mother hearing about it. Whatever change I thought could happen from Riley was futile, and I needed to remember that. There was no way to change things if someone wanted nothing to do with me.

~

"*D*id you see her outfit today?" Priscilla snarked.

Tabitha rolled her eyes. "She's trying to impress the football team." Tabitha leaned in closer. "Too bad she will never be seen that way no matter what she wears."

Priscilla cackled. "Or takes off."

I stared at my lunch. This conversation had lasted fifteen minutes already. I rubbed the back of my neck. Why did they care what someone else wore? Why had we ever cared about any of that? The Vivian Rowe voice in my head said, *"Appearance is your first impression. If you want others to see you, change what you wear."* The automatic saying was enough to make me want to vomit.

"I mean, really, if she wants to fit in, she needs to lose at least ten pounds and maybe color her hair."

"Or get a nose job," Tabitha added.

As Priscilla and Tabitha stayed engrossed in their conversation, I became nauseated—at least they weren't focused on me. I scanned the cafeteria for the familiar table. Across the room sat Riley, Sophie, and Randy. It appeared effortless between them.

I bet they aren't insulting people based on their appearance.

I groaned.

Tabitha and Priscilla stopped talking and stared at me as if I was a freak creature from the ocean's depths.

"You have nothing to say about Mandi's transformation?" Tabitha asked.

I shook my head.

"Seriously, what's wrong with you?" Priscilla asked.

Tabitha's eye twitched, and her smile turned into a sneer. "You know, Priscilla, wouldn't it be interesting if the rest of the school found out about Shelby's little transformation?"

Priscilla sneered. "You know, Tabitha, that's a good point. Shelby, how do you think the rest of Honey Cove High would feel about your *change*?"

I rolled my eyes. "Don't act like you two don't need me. The facts are that my family is more important in this town than both of yours combined. You really want to attack the Rowe empire?"

Tabitha and Priscilla both gasped. "Are you threatening us?"

I glared. "Do I need to?"

They shook their heads.

"We didn't mean it, Shelby," Tabitha said.

"Yeah, we just miss you, is all. It's no fun if we all aren't in on it."

It was an unlikely story. I wasn't naïve enough to believe those two wouldn't throw me under a bus if given the chance. That's how popularity worked. Those who dominated the highest positions had to always look out for themselves, because no one else would.

"There's nothing to miss. I'm merely bored with this conversation. Mandi is a nobody; you two discussing her changes that." I restrained the wince that fought to breakthrough. Those words felt awful to say.

"You're so right, Shelby," Tabitha said.

Priscilla adjusted her smile and leaned closer to me. "What will you do on your break? Any jet-setting adventures?"

"You two know that I have my mother's ball. Plus, when have I ever gone on a jet-setting adventure?"

Tabitha reached for my hand but fell short. "That's so true. You have the best holiday break though. I can't imagine being able to plan a Vivian Rowe ball. It must be so magical to choose."

I batted my lashes and smiled. "Oh yes. It's the best! She lets me watch her spend hours making her decisions. I really get to see such an inside scoop into her creativity."

Priscilla sighed slowly. "That must be wonderful. I wish my mother would throw a party. I can't wait to see what she does. I've had my dress picked out for weeks. What are you wearing, Shelby?"

I wiggled my finger back and forth at them. "Oh no. It's a secret."

In reality, I hadn't even picked mine yet.

Tabitha pouted. "Okay. But I'm sure it's stunning. Not even a small hint? We wouldn't want to show up in the same outfit."

A chuckle escaped my lips. "I highly doubt that."

Priscilla swatted at Tabitha. "Why would you ever think that? You two have never managed to wear the same dress. You don't even have the same body type."

Priscilla trilled on, but I couldn't bear to sustain the conversation. Being fake friendly to them was exhausting, and I would rather do anything else. I stared longingly at Riley's table. What would it feel like to not care what others thought of me? Riley had experienced an extremely embarrassing attack on her and her family, and yet she came out stronger.

She doesn't have my mother though. No. It wasn't a good idea to go down that path. I couldn't change who my parents were, so there was no point in dwelling over it.

The lunch bell rang, and I couldn't be happier to escape this situation. I would have two weeks to figure out what I should do during Christmas break. Tabitha and Priscilla would be at the ball, but it was more manageable. They would be on my turf—more controlled.

I waved to maintain appearances. "Bye, ladies." I made pretend kiss noises and bolted from the lunchroom before they responded.

Sure, we had grown up together, but it was always a competition. Who would win the best hair, nails, boyfriends, Homecoming Court? There was a history, but it wasn't a friendship.

They waved back as I stood from the table and headed toward my locker. I would talk to Riley again, maybe invite her to the ball to apologize. All I had to do was wait until the end of the day, and I would find her. Who wouldn't want to be invited to a ball?

~

*T*he walk to Riley's locker felt wrong. What if she walked away, like she had been doing for months? What if she retaliated? I wasn't really afraid of Riley as much as I hated the guilt I felt when I talked to her. It wasn't okay what Priscilla and Tabitha had done to her, but what I had done was worse. I had stood by, doing nothing. I had known they would escalate when they didn't get their way, and I had known they had found out about Riley's mom.

No, you can't go down that path again. It would have happened one way or another.

I took a deep breath. This was my olive branch; I needed to do it.

Riley and Randy held hands at her locker. They were entranced, staring into each other's eyes.

I had heard rumors they were together, but I knew Randy well enough to know it wasn't as easy as that. He had issues with his family, something I saw firsthand at founders' meetings. How much did Riley really know about how things were?

Riley glanced in my direction as I approached her locker. Her eyes bulged. She released Randy's hand, turned the opposite direction and fled.

The recognition danced across his face until his eyes narrowed, and he stared straight at me—arms crossed.

"I-I didn't want her to run off."

Randy snorted. "I'm sure, but what did you think she would do?"

I sighed. "I just want her to listen to my side."

"Your side? She was really hurt by what was posted about her." He shook his head. "I know you've done some down-right mean things in the past, but damn, Shelby."

"I know." There was no point in denying it anymore. It was my fault, even by association.

"So, why don't you just leave her alone?"

I shrugged. "I don't know. She's different. She doesn't care about this town's founding bullcrap. She is free of those stigmas and expectations. It's envious."

Randy's glare turned into a slight smile. "She is different, and she doesn't need to be sucked in by you and your games. You've tried it before, just leave her alone. You've shown your true colors."

"I don't want everything to be left like that. I came here to invite her to my Christmas ball. I want to include her."

"She isn't going to believe you easily, Shelby. Genuine intentions or not, you broke her trust."

"I see." I eyed him warily. "And you?"

Randy shrugged. "It wasn't me who was embarrassed in front of the entire class on the internet."

"True."

Randy sighed. "I'm on Riley's side with this. We have a lot of history between our families, Shelby, and I know who you are outside these walls, but I won't fight on your behalf."

I played with the strap on my bookbag. "I understand."

Randy turned away.

"Randy?"

He partially faced me. "Yes?"

"Thank you."

"Don't thank me just yet. If you really want to be friends with her, you must figure out how to gain her trust. That won't be easy, and, as long as you act the way you do with your henchmen, she won't believe a word you say."

Was that true? Would I really have to relinquish my façade for Riley to trust me? Could I even do that? This was all I knew. Of course, the mean things I did and said to innocent girls over the years was wrong, but it didn't seem unjust at the time. It was high school. Wasn't that the point? People became tougher for what they endured. I merely helped them be a stronger person. If anything, that was noble, not something I should be tortured for.

I shook my head. What was I saying? Things were so twisted I wasn't sure what voice to listen to anymore.

CHAPTER 2

*P*erfectly manicured lawns surrounded me. The road was windy, but, like everything in our estate, it was well maintained. No part of the yard was left to its own devices.

I rolled my eyes. After everything I had dealt with today, my parents' yard was another reminder to be flawless. I parked in our five-car garage and locked my silver BMW. I approached the house through the back door to avoid the entourage who awaited me. With school officially on break, my mother would expect me to fully participate in the preparations for the ball. The back staircase was near my room and would make it easy to disappear for a few hours.

A rental car blocked my way. Whose car was that? No one in my family would show up in a rental that looked like a Toyota Corolla from the nineties. I squinted at the car then returned to the front of the house.

Most of our guests arrived in expensive limos or in a Rolls Royce. Some guests were picked up at the airport then formally introduced. So to say this car was out of place was an understatement.

I strolled around front and opened the door. It was silent. I peered into the front sitting room then headed toward the ballroom. Whoever was visiting wasn't making a grand entrance.

"Mother, I'm home. Where are you?" I shouted.

There was no answer. It shouldn't be surprising. The house was massive; that's why we had a PA system. But where else would my mother be? She should be perfecting the seating arrangements, choosing china patterns, and having runway shows to choose her extravagant outfit.

Silence made no sense.

Rental cars made no sense.

I climbed the stairs as I contemplated who could be visiting. I wracked my brain, searching for a clue of someone who was expected, but with each stair, I came up empty. I threw open my bedroom's double doors and gasped. I threw my bag on the floor and ran to my bed. "Aunt Delilah!"

Delilah Bryant smiled a large toothy grin that spanned her face. "There's my favorite niece!"

I laughed. "I'm your only niece, Aunt Delilah."

"True, but you're still my favorite. No one said you must like your nieces, especially in this family."

I smiled. "I wasn't expecting you. Mother didn't say anything …" I gasped. "Are *you* the one in the rental car outside?"

Delilah smirked. "Guilty. Your mother hasn't seen it yet. She will *love* that beautiful specimen of a car in her driveway, don't you think?"

I chuckled. "Yeah, after she has a stroke."

Delilah shrugged. "So, how are you? It's been years."

"I'm good. First day of break."

"Oh, how exciting."

"Yep."

Delilah peered at me. "What's wrong?"

"Nothing. It just means I must spend every minute helping Mother with the Christmas ball. You know how she gets."

Delilah rolled her eyes. "Vivian and that blasted thing." She rubbed her chin. "Has it gotten bigger in the last few years? It's been awhile since I've attended one."

I nodded. "This is her fifteenth year, and she's thrilled. I just don't understand why she makes such a big deal about it. It's a party. Why does she have to go all out just because we're a Rowe?"

Delilah smirked and straightened her posture. "Well, you're high society. Appearances must be maintained."

"I guess."

I surveyed the room. "Where are your bags?"

"In the guest room. I chose the green room. It always reminds me of *The Wizard of Oz*."

"I'm surprised Mother hasn't roped you into helping her with planning." I paused. "In fact, I'm surprised I haven't seen her at all yet."

"Well, that's because she doesn't know I'm here. I wanted to surprise her too."

I frowned. "How did you get in?"

Delilah smirked. "I have my ways."

I nudged her elbow. "So, how have you been? I thought you'd be in some fancy apartment in a big city for the holidays."

Aunt Delilah smiled, but it didn't quite make it to her eyes. "I wanted to see you and my sister."

I gave her a quizzical expression. "Yeah, right. You don't enjoy seeing Mother."

"No, but I enjoy seeing you. It's been a few years. You can't blame me for wanting to come visit, can you?"

"Well, no. I'm just surprised. Mother always speaks of you as too busy to come home."

Aunt Delilah's right eyebrow rose. "I'm not sure if I should be more surprised that she discusses me or that she considers me busy!"

I giggled. "She only mentions you if I ask."

"Well, bless you, Shelby, for thinking of me!"

"Of course. You are my favorite aunt."

She winked. "Very true." She rose and smoothed out her sweater and jeans—nothing designer and certainly nothing Vivian Rowe would be caught dead in. "Let's check out this ballroom, shall we?"

We linked arms and walked down the hallway and stairs, talking as we went.

Someone had decorated while I was gone. Wreaths and candles filled every floor-to-ceiling window. Three Christmas trees towered in almost every corner of the room —decorated to match the red and gold color scheme. The tables displayed gold linens. The china and centerpieces weren't placed yet, but I knew they would be on the to-do list.

"Wow," Delilah said. "You weren't kidding."

"See? This isn't even all. In the next couple days, it will only become more extravagant. Wait until you see how she picks our outfits." I pretended to make a gagging noise. "It's so ridiculous. I don't know why she has to make it over the top."

Delilah shrugged. "You know appearances are everything to your mother."

"Yeah, a little too much," I muttered.

A loud bang emanated from the front foyer, followed by the fast-paced clicking sound of heels.

"Who the *hell* is parked outside by the garage?" Vivian shouted in a high-pitched shrill.

Delilah giggled. "Here she comes."

My eyes widened. Only Delilah would take pleasure in

purposely irritating my mother. No one else dared to come close to annoyance. It wasn't pleasant to be on my mother's list, and I certainly never tested it.

"In the ballroom, Mother!"

The clicking became louder as she approached. When she entered the doorway, her brows knitted, and her eyes narrowed. At the sight of her sister, she relaxed a little, but only slightly—imperceptible to most people but not for her daughter.

"*You!*" Vivian crossed her arms. "Delilah, you're driving that piece of junk? Why did you get that? You can afford more than that rental. Or you could have *told* me you were coming, and I would've had a car sent for you."

Delilah's smiled broadened. "And miss this surprise? Not for anything."

"Well, you can't leave it there. You must take it back. Or park by the guesthouse."

"Whatever you say, sister dear."

Vivian shifted her attention to me. "Did you know?"

"Me? No. I was just as surprised as you. I found her sitting on my bed."

Vivian uncrossed her arms. "Well, okay. Look at you. Go change into something more appropriate and come back down. We have people on their way to help choose our outfits for the ball."

I walked past my mother and into the foyer to the sounds of their muffled voices.

~

J delayed my return. I didn't want a million outfits to be paraded in front of me just to choose my attire. It was exhausting and, quite honestly, wasn't ideal for my current mood. I wanted to lay on my bed and rest or spend time with my aunt—anything besides try on clothes.

When I had nothing else to do and wore only what my mother would deem appropriate—a designer knitted sweater dress and calf-high boots—I trudged toward the ballroom. As I approached, I heard raised voices.

"Delilah, be serious. When will you move back and take your life seriously?"

"I do take my life seriously! How dare you say otherwise."

"Oh please, Delilah. You find yourself in these messes every few months then expect other people to clean it up. Or worse, you just leave and let it work itself out. How is that being serious?"

"Vivian—"

I walked through the doorway to the ballroom, and they went silent. They put distance between them. Their faces were reddened.

"I … uh, am ready."

"Splendid. They'll be here momentarily."

Delilah moved closer to the door. "I'll be back. I'm going to freshen up a bit."

"Well, do hurry," Vivian said. "You can look for an outfit for yourself. My treat."

Delilah smiled but her eyes were full of a different emotion. She turned and left.

I shuffled my weight from foot to foot. They had been discussing something serious, and my mother acted haughty as usual. My aunt knew what she was doing with her life; why did my mother have to be so self-righteous? My aunt traveled; how could she not be taking life seriously? I shook my head. I needed to focus. There were plenty of other obstacles I needed to face, and now that my mother was alone, I planned to deal with at least one of them. "So, Mother. I have a question for you."

Vivian focused on the table and didn't look up. "Yes?"

"I was wondering if I could ask you a question about the Christmas ball."

Vivian's posture straightened. She squared her shoulders to face me. Her eyes brightened as she smiled. "Absolutely. I'm glad to see you take interest in the planning."

I twisted the fabric of my dress around my fingers. This wouldn't be the question my mother had in mind, but I had to ask. "I was wondering if I could add another guest to our list?" I paused. "Riley Mills."

Vivian's eyes bulged, and her smile deflated. "Mills? As in the granddaughter of Penny? The one who was conceived out of wedlock?" Vivian shook her head. "Why would you want to formally invite her to our ball? She doesn't belong here."

I tensed. "She's my friend, and I wanted to invite her."

"Your friend? Shelby, what have I always told you? *You are who you associate with.* And that girl is not part of the people I want you to associate with. It's not happening."

I hung my head. I had expected a reaction similar to no, but I didn't realize my mother still held such old-fashioned thinking about the people in this town. Sure, I knew my mother cared about appearances, she had said that same statement many times as I grew up, but things were different —or *should* be different—in this town. Where Riley came from didn't make her any less worthy to attend the ball than any of those *founding families*.

"Come look at your table. Where would I even put her? There can only be eight seats and this table is quite full already."

I trudged to the table my mother mentioned. It had my place card in the calligraphy I had seen earlier that day. On one side of my place card, I saw Tabitha and Priscilla's name, but on the other, I saw a name I wish I hadn't.

"What is *Luke Warrington* doing at this table? And why is he sitting next to me?"

Mother's devilish grin spread across her face. "He's your date. Why wouldn't he be sitting next you?"

Oh my god!

"Mother, really? Why do I have to have a date to your Christmas ball?"

Mother folded her arms. "Because I've told you that's who you will go with."

I frowned. "Why? I didn't have a date last year."

"You also weren't seventeen last year, Shelby. You are a Rowe. Every social appearance is a chance to make a statement."

"And what statement will that make? He's a spoiled boarding school brat."

"Shelby! You best learn a new opinion of that man before my ball. You will not ruin it with that kind of talk."

"How will this *date* look to the people of Honey Cove? He's ridiculous!"

Vivian scowled and folded her arms. "Shelby, I didn't raise you to be that way. Luke Warrington is a perfectly nice young man. He would make a wonderful date to this ball."

Yeah right. On what planet did she think that was true? "This arrangement has nothing to do with me and everything to do with social standing in the community."

Vivian scoffed. "So what if it does, Shelby? You both are part of the founding families. You know we must follow certain important expectations in this family. It's important we show others what founding families can accomplish together. You and Luke being seen together goes a long way toward that goal."

I sighed. "I'm not interested, Mother."

Vivian gripped my arm. "It's not a choice, young lady. You

will have him as your plus-one for the ball. It has already been settled."

The sound of footsteps in the hallway silenced the conversation. People rolled in dresses and set the room for the fashion show.

I lurked near the door.

"Don't you think about disappearing or that I have forgotten your comment. We will talk after this." Vivian narrowed her eyes. "Are we clear?"

I nodded. Of course, it was clear. Everything in my life wasn't my choice. It was a choice made by others about how I should be and the image I was to present. When would it be my turn to have a say in how I lived my life?

CHAPTER 3

I eyed the dresses on the clothes racks. According to my count, this would take way too long to look at all these options.

Delilah arrived back in the ballroom shortly after the last rack of dresses had arrived in the hallway. *Perfect timing.*

"Shelby, we'll start with you. They'll bring them out one by one. If you like it, let us know, and it goes to one rack. If you hate it, then it goes back on their rack. Make sense?" Vivian asked.

"Yes."

This wasn't the first time I had to watch a parade of dresses. For any occasion, this was how we chose. I didn't go to a store like a normal person and pick out something on a rack. My mother ensured I had the best dress possible, which meant flying in options from the biggest cities. It lowered the chance someone could have the same dress, which, of course, my mother thought would be horrendous.

A few people displayed short A-line dresses against their arms. The colors were perfect for the Christmas holidays, but she would never allow me to wear a shorter dress for the ball.

Mother shook her head and stood. "No. Absolutely not. We need long, formal gowns. I specifically asked for all floor-length dresses, nothing short. This isn't some high school dance. We're discussing a formal Christmas ball."

The people nodded furiously and scurried from the room. When they returned, the dresses were longer but weren't right—too many jewels made it look bedazzled, or a slit was way too far up the side.

I wanted understated beauty. I didn't need the glitz and glamour to come from the dress; I wanted it to come from my accessories. I wanted simple, elegant. I dismissed another several dresses. I stared at my rack then at my mother. If something wasn't moved to the rack soon, she would get annoyed. She wouldn't assume I was browsing for the right one. She would assume I was being difficult on purpose. Especially after my comments in regard to attending the ball with Luke.

Ugh, even the thought of his name made me cringe. I had been lucky to only be around him for a few minutes every other year, but even then, he was unbearable.

A deep red mermaid dress with laced sleeves was the first one in the next set. It wasn't the right one, but it was doable if I got stuck with it.

"You can move that one to the rack," I said as I pointed to it.

Mother's frown lessened and turned more into a polite grin. It worked in lightening her mood, which would go a long way. "Very nice."

Aunt Delilah put up her thumbs as she sat quietly. Something was off with her demeanor. She was either bored or was still chewing on my mother's earlier comments. Either way, until this extravagant charade ended, we would all have to sit and deal with it.

Another several dresses were displayed, and in the very back was a hunter-green one. I rose and approached the dress. It was perfect. The color was exactly what I wanted this year for the holidays, and it was the right length. I grabbed the hanger from the woman and brought it toward the front.

Once in the light, I saw it was an off-the-shoulder style with a beaded rhinestone bodice. It would hug my hourglass figure and look phenomenal with the planned accessories. "This one. This is perfect."

Delilah gave me a thumbs up, and Mother smiled.

"Perfect choice, Shelby. I'll let Luke know the color is hunter green."

I smiled through gritted teeth. "Thanks, Mother. Now your turn."

Mother clapped. "Actually, I think Delilah should go next."

Delilah's expression tightened. She clearly didn't enjoy choosing dresses. She waved her hand in front of her face. "No, I couldn't possibly. Why don't you, Vivian? The host should have first choice. You must look perfect."

Vivian stroked her chin as she considered this. "You're right. Okay, you can choose after me. Although, if you see something you absolutely love, just let me know."

"Of course."

"Wonderful. Okay let's see the selection for the adults, shall we?" Vivian peered at one of the women still holding the dresses for me. She narrowed her eyes as they stayed still. "Today!"

They gathered the remaining junior dresses and scurried from the room. They wheeled in a new rack containing several dress options.

Mother scrutinized each choice, running her fingers over the fabric, then rudely threw them at people.

I rolled my eyes. She was so dramatic. Why couldn't she just be normal or at least treat people with respect? This was their job. She could at least be nice about it.

I caught a glimpse of my aunt from the corner of my eye. Delilah gestured her head toward the hallway, and I nodded. It was as good a time as any to quickly sneak out. Vivian would be engrossed in her dress options, and we could escape.

Once in the hallway, I exhaled.

"I just needed some air," Delilah said.

"I understand. She gets intense with these stupid fashion shows. Why can't we just go somewhere and look at dresses?"

Delilah shrugged. "You know your mother."

"Are you okay? I only caught a little bit of your conversation earlier."

Delilah huffed. "I'm fine, really. Your mother is always full of opinions. Nothing out of the ordinary."

"Very true."

"Who's this date you're taking? Anybody dreamy?"

I snorted. "Yeah, right. Luke Warrington is the son of a founding family, and she wants us to show how we can manage things together if we all show a united front. It's some political ploy."

"Ah, one of those."

"Exactly. I would rather go alone, but it's not up to me. I have no choice in the matter."

"Did you have an alternative?"

"No. She wouldn't listen to it. If it's not a founding family, she doesn't care. Luke is the only one not with someone right now. Imagine that."

Delilah chuckled. "I'm sure he's wonderful."

I rolled my eyes. "Wonderful at being a jerk, sure. He goes to boarding school and is generally absent in all things Honey Cove, but of course he must attend the ball of the year."

"Well, maybe it won't be as bad as you think. Let's get back, and maybe we can hurry along your mother. We wouldn't want her to notice us missing, and I am absolutely famished."

I hadn't paid much attention to what time it was, but Aunt Delilah was right; it was dinnertime, and my stomach also gurgled in anticipation. As I crept back into the room, I noticed my mother still scowling and yelling at the people in the room. I rubbed my temples and sat. This would be a long night.

~

It had indeed droned on for two more hours before Vivian gave up and flung more hangers at the poor people. Delilah never had a chance to even look for herself because Vivian was too upset about the whole thing.

I wanted to disappear by the second time someone cried. It ended on such a dreadful note.

I stared at my mother and my aunt. They couldn't be more different, in this moment and in their lives. Even if Mother felt superior, I was sure my aunt had more class. Yelling at workers never felt okay.

Delilah stuck out her tongue at me.

I giggled and sat, waiting to be released.

"Absolutely incompetent," Mother muttered. "Couldn't follow a single direction. I wanted ballgowns, not mid-calf dresses. Honestly, some people should not be in the people-pleasing industry."

I restrained from rolling my eyes. How did my mother not hear the words she uttered?

"I'm sure you'll find something," Delilah said.

"Well, I have to, don't I? I can't arrive to my own ball in my undergarments. That would be absurd."

Delilah stifled a laugh. "Now that would be a sight."

"Oh, come off it, Delilah. This is serious."

Delilah waved off Mother. "Everything is so serious to you. It's an outfit. You'll find something. It's not a big deal."

Vivian stomped her foot. "It absolutely is. This is the fifteenth year. I can't just pull something from my closet, Delilah. You know that."

Delilah rolled her eyes. "Of course, how silly of me to forget. What the queen wants, the queen gets."

Vivian narrowed her eyes at her sister. "Excuse me?"

Delilah stood straighter. "You heard me. You were absolutely horrific to those hard workers. Even if they had misunderstood what you wanted, you didn't have to scream at them like a raving lunatic. Where is your class?"

Vivian crossed her arms and stared at her sister.

I shuddered.

My mom used her icy stare, reserved only for those who royally infuriated her. "I'll have you know I have plenty of class. I did them a favor. The commission those people could have made from the three dresses I would have bought would have made their monthly revenue. You can't coddle people when they screw up. That does no one any good. They learned their lesson, and I'm sure they won't misunderstand me again."

Delilah threw her hands in the air. "Because it's all about you? What if they had unforeseen circumstances in their lives, and you just crapped all over them? Have some decency. They are people too, and just because you have money and some old-money name doesn't make you better. Or do you forget we are *both* Bryants?"

Mother huffed. "I remember where I'm from, and I was perfectly appropriate. You can find your own damn dress."

"Fine."

"Fine." Mother stomped toward the staircase, her shoes clicking as she went. When she reached the doorway, she stopped. "Shelby, you need to be up early, so go to bed now. Your father expects you in the foyer at seven o'clock tomorrow for the founders' meeting."

"Okay."

Mother stalked off and didn't look back.

I unhinged my fingers from my side; fingernail marks etched my skin. I walked toward my aunt. "Are you okay?"

Delilah shrugged. "I'll be fine. This is normal. I'm glad you found a dress. I need to rest, and, as your mother said, you must be up early. I'll see you tomorrow."

"Are you sure? You haven't even eaten yet. We could get Frank the chef to make us food. He won't mind."

"No, thank you. I'm exhausted, and I'm afraid she has stolen my appetite. Why don't you still get food, and I'll see you tomorrow."

I watched as Delilah went in the opposite direction of Mother toward the back stairs through the kitchen. I sighed. Their fight had been intense. Mother wouldn't be in a better mood by tomorrow. She didn't forgive and forget. She was prone to holding a grudge.

I stared at the beautiful hunter-green dress, turned off the lights in the ballroom and trudged to the kitchen. "Frank!"

Chef Frank strolled around the kitchen wall and stood in front of the counter.

He was a muscular and tall gentleman, not resembling what I pictured chefs to look like. I always imagined chefs were rotund because of all the food they cooked, but he wasn't. He kept himself in shape, regardless of his occupation. "Yes? What can I make you?"

"I'm so sorry to bother you, but I am starving."

Chef Frank smiled. "It's my job, so no problem. What are you in the mood for?"

"What about some pasta?"

"Anything in particular?"

"Nope. Just surprise me."

Chef Frank winked. "Can do. I'll have it ready in twenty."

I sat at the dining room table. As I waited, the memories of the day flooded back to me. How could I get Tabitha and Priscilla to either change or leave me alone? And what happened to Aunt Delilah that had made Mother go off on her like that?

My phone sat in front of me, and finally, as a distraction to my circling thoughts, I checked my messages. It had been on silent the entire time we had to choose outfits. My mother would have gone ballistic if it had gone off.

Unfortunately, my messages carried no distraction. It was absolutely empty of unread messages. No one had checked to see how my night went. Tabitha and Priscilla may have appeared to be my best friends, but, in truth, it was all a competition. Any word of weakness and they would use it against me.

My fingers drummed against the table as I waited. Smells of pasta sauces wafted from the stove as Chef Frank cooked. He was a fabulous chef. So far, he had been employed at the Rowe Estate for five years. I knew we'd employed other chefs before him but none I remembered quite like Chef Frank. He looked out for me, even in this massively large house and despite being an employee.

I watched Chef Frank as he floated around the kitchen. Pots and pans piled high into the large stainless-steel sink. He whistled and hummed while he worked, a habit my mother hated. She felt staff should do their jobs without being seen or heard.

Chef Frank carried a plate to where I sat. "Here you go, madam."

The smells from the plate filtered into my nostrils and left me sighing in contentment. His meals were always fabulous; anyone who chose to go to bed on an empty stomach was a fool.

"Thank you so much, Chef Frank."

He beamed. "You're welcome, Shelby. Anything else I can make you?"

I shook my head. "I'm good. I think everyone else went to sleep. You can probably knock off for the night."

"Goodnight, Shelby. I will see you in the morning. If you need anything, make sure to buzz."

"I will! Goodnight, Chef Frank."

The pasta slipped off my fork as I tried to twirl it around the tines. I took a bite and smacked my lips. It was fabulous. He had made alfredo, one of my favorites. I enjoyed most sauces, but ones made from tomatoes didn't sit quite the same for me, and Chef Frank knew it. He was amazing.

The pasta was gone faster than I would have liked, but I rinsed off the plate and headed for my room. It would be an early morning, and I needed to be rested for any kind of meeting involving my father. He didn't enjoy weakness, especially not from his own family.

CHAPTER 4

I stared at the empty chair on my right in the meeting room. Most of the founders and some of their first-born children were already at the meeting but not Thaddeus Rowe. Of course, as the top-founding family, he had to make a grand entrance, but he was never late. I checked my phone for the third time. He wasn't technically late yet, but he usually arrived earlier than this to meetings.

Through the door strolled Randy Walker and his father, Silas.

I gave a slight wave, but Randy didn't pay attention.

He stood a foot or two in front of his father who had a slumped posture and dark circles under his eyes. His clothes looked disheveled, and he overall had an unkempt appearance. Silas didn't look good. The stories in town were mostly contained, but it was obvious that man had a problem.

To avoid staring, I diverted my gaze.

Priscilla's uncle sat at the end of the table with Tabitha's grandfather next to him. Both of those men were as judgmental as Tabitha and Priscilla. It wasn't a wonder why they both acted the way they did.

What was I saying? My parents weren't saints either and, in most circles, neither was I.

Just as the clock chimed, Thaddeus Rowe strutted through the door. "Good morning, everyone. Glad to see you all made it this close to Christmas." He smiled at the other members as he passed then winked at me.

I smiled, although it was the furthest from my real emotions. Why had he waited until the minute the meeting was to start to arrive? He had asked me to be ready then sent a car. Why didn't he drive us both to the meeting?

"Today's agenda is shorter than usual, but with the holidays, we need laser focus."

Thaddeus trailed on with the agenda, but I couldn't concentrate. I didn't care what a bunch of stuffy old men had to discuss. I wanted these meetings to be about something, but they rarely were what I had in mind. Not to mention, I was the first female to sit at this table. If I'd had a different father, I had no doubt it would have never happened. But since I was Thaddeus Rowe's only child, I received special privileges. Even so, it was limited. The other families' patriarchs saw me as a beautiful face not to be heard.

I watched Randy, who listened intently to my father. He seemed good, happier since meeting Riley. Another person changed from knowing Riley Mills. Randy had been a loner after he quit baseball and stopped caring about his image. While they weren't officially together, Randy seemed more of his old self since Riley had entered the picture—despite his father's indiscretions around town.

My father turned toward me. "Shelby will help us."

Crap, what was I helping with? I had been so consumed in my thoughts I missed what had happened. I smiled and nodded, hoping there was a clue somewhere.

Mr. Tate, Priscilla's older uncle, spoke up from the other end of the table. "And how exactly can a little girl help us?"

He was a squat man—short and bald. He had no heirs, which was a shame. The position at the table would go to Priscilla's family eventually when it was deemed for him to step down.

Thaddeus smirked. "This *little* girl is almost a senior in high school and what better way for us to take hold in the younger generation than with someone who knows what they're thinking."

"I'm not convinced she can help us. We don't need ideas about dresses and gowns. We need serious ways to get more tourism to our town and to increase the revenue. We still haven't recovered our losses from when the bee populations declined."

Thaddeus folded his hands. "Shelby is more than qualified to help get tourists. She knows her generation. Let her come up with something and show you."

The other board members sat in contemplation. Most of their faces contorted into a frown or confused expression. Based on looks alone, they certainly didn't seem to think I could do it.

I searched for Luke Warrington's father. What would my date's parents think about the idea?

Thomas Warrington was tall even while he sat at the table. His short golden-brown hair styled to the side accentuated his honey-colored eyes against his light complexion. His face, like many of the others, was unreadable.

I gulped. "Absolutely. I can have something ready in a few weeks," I lied. What on earth did I know about marketing or drawing up proposals? Sure, I had seen my father do those things with investors at his company, but I was never in charge.

Silas Walker stood albeit swaying ever so slightly. He cleared his throat. "My son Randy could certainly help Shelby as well. He has helped with our company in the last few years, and we have seen several gains in our profits from the changes he has made."

Thaddeus raised his hand. "I appreciate your offer, Silas, but Shelby can do it."

I put my hand over my father's. "I would be willing to hear other opinions. Let Randy consult on the project."

My father's lips tightened as he searched my face. After a small hesitation, he nodded. "Okay, it's settled. We will reconvene in one week after the Christmas festivities. I will see you all at the ball."

The chairs scooted toward the walls as everyone stood and filtered from the entryway.

Randy waved at me then followed his father out.

My father was in a heavy discussion with the mayor, which meant I would have time to catch Randy before he left.

I squeezed around Mr. Warrington, Mr. Tate, and Mr. Richards clogging the walkway in heated discussions. Randy and his father were just up ahead.

I jogged toward them until I was closer. "Randy," I whispered.

Randy stopped and faced me. His eyebrows scrunched together. "Did I forget something?"

"No. I wanted to catch you before you left."

"Oh." He eyed his father. "About what?"

"It will only take a minute."

"Dad, I'll be right back. Meet you at the car?"

Silas smiled and doffed his hat. He turned toward the front of the building and kept walking.

I ran my fingers over my shirt, playing with the bow strings toward the bottom. "I really am excited to work with you on this project."

Randy crossed his arms. "What's this about, Shelby? I have a busy day."

"Of course. I wanted to tell you I tried to get Riley an invitation to my mother's ball, but she wouldn't budge."

Randy smiled. "That's it?"

I frowned. "You aren't upset I couldn't get her in?"

"No. She's been on the guestlist for a month. She's my plus-one. Now, if that's all you wanted to say, I need to go."

"Wait. She's coming?"

"Yes, with me."

"Oh, well, that's great. I'm glad."

"Yes, but I do really need to go." He turned and left the hallway toward the parking lot.

What had just happened? That wasn't how I had planned anything. If he had already found a way for Riley to go, why hadn't he mentioned it when I had said something at the lockers? It would have saved me the headache of asking my mother. Not to mention that was my olive branch. I wanted her to think she could trust me, but without a true invitation, what would I use now?

I shook my head and returned to the meeting room.

My father shook hands with Mr. Taylor as he left. The Taylors were one of the families who had managed to buy their way onto the founding council. As the head of an insanely wealthy family, Mr. Taylor managed to stay humble in his decisions—one of the few on the council.

We were alone when my father frowned at me. "Why did you take help on that proposal? Especially from the Walker boy?"

I shrugged. "It seemed like a good idea."

"No. It wasn't. That family is already on a tightrope. We don't need you two spending time together. What will people say?"

I rolled my eyes internally. Outwardly, I grinned and, through gritted teeth, said, "Nothing. Not when they see my date to the ball."

Thaddeus's facial muscles relaxed. "Who might that be?"

"Mother set me up with Luke."

His expression was unreadable.

"Warrington. Luke Warrington."

Father smiled. "Ah, good family. And very true. Okay, you can meet one time, but you aren't to take any of his ideas, Shelby. Are we clear?"

I nodded. My parents always told me what to do. My mother demanded I wear this outfit or look this way, while my father forced me to take proposals and make negotiations with certain families. Either way, they worried about the same thing—the family name and legacy, never what I wanted.

"Father, where were you this morning?"

"Hmm?" he said as he checked his phone, absorbed in his messages, emails, or anything besides me.

"This morning, you came separately."

"Oh, I had business to handle. That's all." He finished typing something then shoved his phone into his suit pants' pocket. "Shall we go?"

I nodded but kept silent. Why did no one pay attention to what I wanted? They used me as a pawn but not as their daughter.

~

*H*alf an hour later, we pulled into our long winding driveway. My father remained silent. He stared at his phone, and I stared out the window. I learned early that it was best to stay quiet until he initiated a conversation.

The driver pulled the vehicle to the front door and parked.

We climbed out and walked to the front door, Father in the lead.

In the entrance way stood Mother and Aunt Delilah. Mother smiled at the sight of her husband. "Ah, Thad, I'm glad you're home. We've missed you." She approached Thaddeus and attempted to hug him, but he sideswiped her advance. She frowned but quickly recovered at the sight of me.

Aunt Delilah slouched on the front step of the grand staircase and tipped her head. "Thaddeus." She didn't smile, and the crinkle by her eyes when she laughed was absent. Her expression was devoid of emotion, as if meeting a stranger. But even strangers were welcomed with more emotion than that.

Thaddeus nodded toward Delilah, not making eye contact. "Yes, well, I can't stay. I have another business trip I must take."

Mother's eyes bulged. "A business trip? Thaddeus, it's December twenty-first, and you're leaving? When do you return?"

"December twenty-fourth."

Her shoulders slumped as she tried to steady herself against the stair railing. "The twenty-fourth? *Christmas Eve?* But that's the night of the ball! You must be there." She fanned herself. "What will people say if you're not there?"

"Relax, Vivian. I'll be home in time. No one will know or say anything."

She tried to compose herself. She straightened the jacket she had over her dress. "I … I can make it work." She narrowed her gaze. "You promise you'll be home in time?"

"Yes," Thaddeus said and climbed the staircase toward the bedroom without another word.

Delilah snorted. "How convenient."

"Delilah not now," Vivian said as she squeezed the bridge of her nose.

"When is the time, Vivian? He leaves you alone all the time. What is so important he needs to be gone for the next three days? Companies are closed. No one does business at this point in the year."

"That's not true."

"Yes, it is. Wake up and actually look at this situation. He does nothing for you and Shelby."

My mouth fell open. This wasn't a conversation I wanted to witness. Nor did I think my mother would handle the comments very well. Mother was stressed out enough; she didn't need a fight with her sister either. It would put everyone on edge.

Vivian's head flew up, and her eyes narrowed. "How dare you? He puts a roof over our head and makes sure we want for nothing. That is a whole lot more than nothing."

Delilah scoffed. "Sure, but where's the love? Where's the attention? You and Shelby certainly can't connect to someone who is like a ghost in this house."

Vivian crossed her arms and stomped to Delilah. "That man does more than you will ever know. This conversation is over." Vivian spun to face me. "And you need to get changed. You're expected at the barn."

I raced up the stairs. I would muck out the stalls myself if it meant I wasn't present for another second of their fight. Nothing good would come from it, and I didn't want to be considered an accessory.

CHAPTER 5

I quickly changed and raced from the house. Whatever was wrong with my mother and my aunt, I didn't need to be present for it. Going riding would be a nice distraction. I always forgot my responsibilities while I rode my horse, Rio. I had to focus on my posture and the feel of my saddle which let everything else fade away.

The walk to the stable wasn't too long, especially not when I was distracted by my thoughts. I needed a plan to deal with my unwanted suitor for the ball and on how to make Riley forgive me or at least drift in that direction.

I tightened my light jacket around my arms more securely. A brisk wind blew across the field. My ride would be a little colder than I enjoyed, but it was better than staying in the house.

I stared at the massive white stables in front of me. The edges donned metal molded in intricate patterns. Even buildings were adorned with wealth and beauty in the Rowe estate. Money was a ticket to Honey Cove, and my parents ensured everyone in town knew just how much they had.

The large front entrance to the stable had double doors—

37

perfect for traffic with the horses. Even though I was the only one with my own horse, the rest of the stables were full. Each stall was rented at a high cost and, of course, only to particular townspeople. Not just anyone could rent a stall at Rowe Stables, only privileged families or Rowe Industries coworkers.

I sighed and entered the stables. The stalls were full, with most of the horses in for feeding. Rio didn't stay in the front with the horses who rented their space. He had his own section in the back.

I patted my pockets, looking for my riding gloves, just as I smacked right into the back of someone—someone who suddenly became familiar as a whiff of cologne invaded my nostrils.

"Luke," I muttered.

Luke turned and faced me as a broad smile spread across his face. "Ah, just who I was looking for."

I narrowed my eyes. "Well, this is my stable, and that would be my horse, so A-plus for your sleuthing abilities."

"How nice. You're happy to see me too."

"Not really. Luke, what do you want?" I crossed my arms. "I'm about to go for a ride. Don't you have boarding school friends to see on your break?"

He stepped forward, overshadowing me. "Me too, and the only person I need to see is you."

"What? You're not going on a ride with me."

"But I am. It's scheduled." He thrusted his phone displaying an email toward me. "Right there. Eleven-thirty ride with Shelby Rowe."

"You sent that to yourself."

Luke shook his head. "Actually, no. Your mother invited me."

I held in my sigh. Of course, she invited Luke. Why wouldn't she? It was the perfect ploy, and I couldn't get out of it. Only, I didn't want my ride ruined by the likes of Luke. He was haughty and arrogant, and I wanted nothing to do with him. It was bad enough to be forced together at the ball; who on earth would see us out riding?

"Well, I don't care. I'm riding Rio on my own."

"On your own with me. You can't get rid of me that easily."

I gripped the door to Rio's stall. "What is it you want, exactly? This can't be your ideal first day of Christmas break."

"Maybe not, but who would turn down time with the prettiest girl in Honey Cove?"

I huffed. "Whatever, Luke. If you want to come along, you better keep up."

"Fine by me."

I took Rio from his stall and saddled him up. I vaguely checked if Luke did the same with a different horse, but I didn't care. I wasn't waiting. I walked Rio from the stables and used the stepstool to pull myself onto the saddle. I patted his mane and grabbed the reins.

I knew I should start slow and let Rio warm up before I went too hard, but I wanted to run. The faster I rode, the more distance would be between me and Luke. I pulled back the reins and kicked hard. Rio shot into the pasture, and I kept my eyes peeled forward, hair blowing in the wind under my helmet.

I didn't turn around. I didn't stop, and I didn't care. If he was still there when I slowed down, then good for him. If not, he didn't belong out there anyway.

*M*y breath was quick. I barely slowed the entire ride. It had been awhile since I maintained that pace, and both of us felt it. I patted Rio's neck as we slowed to enter the ring outside the stable. His neck and mane were sweaty. He deserved a good bath and some oats once I was done. I lead Rio into his stable willingly. Shortly after he was secured with some hay and oats, Luke strolled into the stable with the horse he borrowed. My eyes narrowed. He had managed to keep up from what I could tell, but I didn't like it and certainly didn't want to give him a chance to talk to me much.

"Someone likes a fast pace," Luke said.

"What, couldn't keep up?"

Luke scoffed. "I kept up just fine." He shortened the distance between us. "It wasn't the ride I had in mind though."

"Well, too bad." I put my saddle and gear in the tack room ignoring Luke as much as possible. When I left the room, he stood right in the way.

"Can you please leave, Luke? You had your ride, schedule maintained. There's no reason for you to stay."

"Why, of course there is. We were supposed to discuss our arrangement on the horse ride, but since you refused to do anything but flee, we have to talk now."

I groaned. "About what? I'm sure my mother has it all planned and has already delivered it to your people."

"Surely, but that's not what I mean."

"What else is there?"

Luke gestured between us. "This. Us. We must feel like a couple for it to work."

"I don't have to do anything, just so we're clear."

Luke sneered. "Well, that's not entirely accurate. You need to make this believable, or neither of our families will be happy. And honestly, this is not believable. You look and act icy toward me. How are people to believe we're in love?"

I laughed. "In love? Get real. I will be friendly when the time comes, but until then, I don't want to see you."

"That just won't do—"

"What exactly won't do?" Delilah glared at Luke then faced me. "Is this boy bothering you, Shelby?"

I shook my head. "Luke was just leaving. Weren't you?"

"Not exactly."

I glared at him. "Yes, you are. We'll talk about the ball later."

Luke began to speak then stopped and nodded. He turned around and walked away from us.

"Who was that boy?" Delilah asked.

"My *date* for Mother's Christmas ball."

"Oh, what a peach he is."

"Yeah, tell me about it. Mother scheduled a ride for me with Luke without even telling me. She needs to stop pushing it."

Delilah sighed. "I understand that all too well. What do you say we ditch this stuffy stable and go do something fun?"

I smiled. "Like what?"

"You'll just have to wait and see."

∼

I stared at the large, open room containing multiple folding tables and chairs with four people sitting at each table. My eyes bulged when I saw the decks of cards.

"Is this …?"

"A room full of people playing cut-throat pinochle? Yes!" Delilah replied.

"Oh my gosh! I haven't seen this many people play at once before. How did you know about this?"

Delilah winked. "I have my ways. Let's grab two seats at an empty table."

I followed Delilah around the tables and toward the back to a table where all four seats weren't occupied. I sat in a chair next to Delilah.

"No. Across from me."

"But why? How am I going to get help?"

"Don't you remember? We must sit across from each other to be on the same team. And don't worry, it's just for fun."

I sat across from her instead. I surveyed the large fire hall. It had been converted with ease, which only meant this was done frequently. How had I never known this was here?

Because Mother would have never allowed it, that's why.

Most of the people were women in their upper fifties and sixties. Delilah and I had to be the youngest ones in the whole room. But I didn't mind. It meant less people to focus on the fact that a Rowe sat in a fire hall, playing pinochle.

My mother would lose her ever-loving mind if she found out Delilah had brought me here. She absolutely hated card games—especially being a female in the Rowe empire. I could hear her now: *"This is unbecoming of a Rowe, Shelby!"*

Well, maybe for once I didn't want to be a Rowe. I wanted to be myself.

Only a few minutes passed before two older ladies who seemed to be friends took the seats to the left and right of me. I took a deep breath to calm my nerves, until the woman to my left faced me, and I nearly choked. It was Penny Brooks, Riley's mom-mom. *Oh no, no, no.*

"Welcome, ladies. I'm glad you could join us. My niece and I are learning. She is a novice, and I must admit, I don't get a chance to play too often," Delilah said. "We are very excited to play a game or two."

Penny smiled at Delilah, completely oblivious of who we were.

I eyed Delilah to try and warn her, but it was no use. She would have no idea this was not who we wanted to play cards with.

"Well, that is so kind of you. This is Estella, and I'm Penny. What are your names?"

I squeezed my eyes closed, hoping it would magically transport me somewhere else.

"My name's Delilah, and my niece is Shelby."

I peeked at Penny's face and held a breath.

Penny's eyes widened as she stared. She turned to my aunt and smiled. "Very nice to meet you both. What beautiful names." She touched her chin. "Are we ready to begin?"

Phew! I unclenched my fingers and sighed. That would have been bad. For whatever reason, I was blessed she had no idea who I was. I didn't know why I was so lucky, but I would take it.

I watched as Penny and Estella shuffled the deck and dealt our hands. Butterflies erupted in my stomach and made me uneasy. I wasn't prepared to play for the first time in years with Riley's mom-mom. If I did horrible, Riley would know. If I was rude or anything unpleasant, she would know.

What would I do?

Delilah met my gaze and winked. She mouthed, *Breathe, you'll do fine.* She arranged her cards in her hand and looked up. "For both of our sakes, can we get a refresh of the rules perhaps?"

"Absolutely," Estella said. "Once you have your hands ready, you need to count your meld. Meld is the points you gain when you have certain cards. For example, aces around are ten points. Once you count your meld, the person to the left of the dealer, which would be Delilah since Penny dealt, bids. You can go up by ones or make jumps, depending on your meld. If you have low meld and don't have a strong run to make trump, you can pass."

I nodded, trying to retain all the new words Estella threw at us. Some were familiar, but others were brand new. "I have a question."

"Of course," Estella said.

"What's trump?"

"Good point. Trump is the suit chosen by the winner of the bid. The trump card can win if it's played when someone runs out of a suit. However, if someone leads with trump, then you must go higher to win the hand. The order for cards are ace, ten, king, queen, jack. We don't use the nines."

Delilah peered over her hand and scrunched her nose.

I had no idea what that meant or if she was bluffing.

"Is it possible we can play a practice hand, just so we can adjust?" Delilah asked.

Estella and Penny exchanged looks then nodded.

"Perfect," Delilah said.

I stared at the cards one by one as I picked them up off the table. I arranged them in suits then in order, although it was strange to think of a ten being higher than a king.

Penny grabbed a folded piece of paper from her bag and pushed it toward me. "Use this to help count your meld. It's a cheat sheet of the hands you could have and how many points."

I grabbed the paper and moved it closer. "Thank you."

Penny stared back at her hand.

Delilah wiggled in her seat and cleared her throat. "Fifty-one."

Estella stared at her cards and eyed Penny. They had formulated some kind of signal, but I had no idea how to read it. I focused on my cards.

According to the paper, I had kings around, which I assumed was a king in each suit, and double pinochle, which was two queens of spades, and two jacks of diamonds, at least that was what the paper said. I had nothing else, and my hand was skewed all over the place. It really didn't concentrate on anything, which I assumed meant a poor hand.

"Fifty-three," Estella said.

I sighed. I had no idea what I should do. I didn't think I could really do much with my hand. If I was supposed to have high cards, I certainly didn't. Too many jacks would get me nowhere, and I was missing one to have jacks around, so I couldn't even use it in my meld bid. I stared at Delilah and hoped she understood. "I pass."

Penny smirked. "Fifty-four."

Delilah shuffled a few cards here and there but folded them and placed it on the table. "Pass."

"Fifty-five," Estella said.

"You can have it," Penny answered.

Estella smirked. "Trump is hearts." She laid cards on the table. "Now that we finished bidding, we have to set down any meld we have to show the rest of the table. If you don't have more than twenty as a team though, you don't set it down. If you have aces around, you have to say that though."

"Aunt Delilah, I think we need to put it down. I have thirty-eight by myself."

"Thirty-eight! Why didn't you tell me?"

"Is that good?"

Delilah smirked. "Yes!"

Estella and Penny nodded.

"That kind of meld score is helpful for your partner to know. Sometimes you need to know so you don't pass. The only way to get points is to keep your meld and make twenty points in the actual game. If you do that, you get to keep the meld points," Penny said.

"Oh, I didn't know. But I thought if I didn't have a big run or anything, I shouldn't bid."

Penny set her cards on the table, revealing three marriages, two of which were in Estella's trump. "Not necessarily. Yes, that does have to be a factor, because having a lot of points and nothing to protect it with gets messy, but you have a partner. Between you both, you need the muscle. If your partner doesn't know what you have, they may not bid, but bidding appropriately will let them know you might have some points they can work with."

"That makes sense. So, how do I tell my partner I had that many points?"

"It varies between partners. It helps to have a system, but most usually show how much meld they have in their bid. For example, did you see that I jumped two when I bid over your aunt?" Estella asked.

I nodded.

"That told Penny I had at least twenty meld. She knows I have something to work with and then she could let me know how much she had. If it got back around to us, we could have kept going if she really wanted it because of her hand. It's a balance."

I set my double pinochle and kings onto the table. "That makes sense." I surveyed the rest of the cards on the table. Estella had a run in her trump in addition to queens, while Penny had three marriages and aces. This didn't look good. I checked Delilah's hand. She also had aces and a marriage in trump. Maybe it wouldn't be so bad after all.

"Okay, grab your cards, and now Estella starts, because she called trump. She can lead with whatever card she wants. You go next, Shelby. Whatever suit she puts down, you must choose a card higher than hers in that suit. If you don't have anything higher, you can tie. If you have none of that suit, you play trump, which is hearts," Penny said.

I waited for Estella to go.

She played a queen of spades. "No, you go," Estella said.

I stared at my hand. What should I put down? I didn't have many high cards. I settled for a king of spades and waited for Penny to go.

Penny smirked and plopped down an ace of spades.

Delilah frowned and used a king too.

"Juicy," Estella said.

I scrunched my nose. "Why is it *juicy?*"

"In this part of the game, ace, ten, and kings count as one point each. So you and your aunt gave us a point for that hand, plus the ace from me," Penny said.

"Oh, and this is when we need twenty points?"

They all nodded.

Delilah smiled and winked at me. I was glad she had convinced them to do a practice hand. There were a lot of rules to remember.

The hand went around and around until we were finally out of cards. I felt like I was along for the ride, but I watched Penny and Estella as they worked. I could tell they had been partners for years, from their silent communication.

"Nicely done, Shelby. Not bad for your first real hand," Delilah said.

"Thanks, Aunt Delilah. This is fun."

I watched as Delilah and Estella shuffled the cards. Penny stole glances toward me. I couldn't help but wonder if she realized who I was. I hoped she hadn't, because I was enjoying myself.

Delilah dealt the cards.

I slowly collected them and added them to my hand.

Penny looked up and met my gaze. "Yanno, Shelby is a beautiful name. My granddaughter knows a girl in her high school class named Shelby. Any ideas?"

My cheeks reddened. I stared at my cards intently, burning a hole into the material. *Oh no, this is exactly what I didn't want to happen.* I gulped. "Your granddaughter is Riley Mills, right?"

Penny's gaze narrowed. "That's her."

"I know Riley. I'm Shelby Rowe."

I watched Penny react to my last name. It wasn't possible that Penny had no idea who I was. After what Riley had endured the past few months, I had a funny feeling Penny knew it all. Or at least enough to make things uncomfortable.

Penny donned a smile. "I'll let her know I saw you here today, Shelby. She will certainly want to know I saw you, *darlin'*." Penny's southern drawl accentuated *darlin'* in the way I knew meant the same as a threat. It was a very subtle way for her to stick knives in my stomach and twist.

Aunt Delilah scrunched her nose and scowled.

I shook my head. I knew better than to touch any of that with a ten-foot pole. All my hopes of having a fun afternoon playing cards went down the drain with that comment.

How did I always end up in these predicaments?

CHAPTER 6

I stayed silent as Penny shuffled the two decks then stowed them in their proper cartons. We had lost at pinochle—both games—but that was okay. I had learned a lot more about pinochle than I thought I ever would, and I had managed to have fun even though Penny certainly discovered I was *that* Shelby Rowe.

My aunt had tried to pry the information from me during our brief intermission between games, but Estella never left, and I refused to discuss it in front of mixed company. It was my fault that Penny knew my name in a negative way. I had been awful to Riley, even if it was unintentional.

I scooted the chair from the table and cringed when it screeched.

Penny stared into my eyes then gently grabbed my arm. "Shelby, could I talk to you for a moment?"

I shifted my gaze between her and my aunt who was still trying to decide if she needed to save me or let it be.

I shook my head at my aunt. "Sure."

Penny gestured to the side of the table away from my aunt and Estella and the other tables wrapping up their game. Penny crossed her arms. "Now, I know you know who I am, and I know you realize I've figured out who you are as well, but I can't help wonder how a girl who sat and played pinochle the way you did today would act the way you did before."

My jaw slackened. Whatever I had expected Penny to say certainly was not that. "Mrs. Brooks—"

"Penny, please."

"Penny … I don't know how to answer that entirely."

Penny's eyebrow rose. "Try your best."

I fidgeted with my clutch purse and stared at my feet then met her gaze. "What happened to Riley was terrible, and any and all parts I added to it, I feel horrible about. I stand by what I told your granddaughter—or have tried to tell her. I didn't know about Tabitha's and Priscilla's intentions. I didn't see the post until the damage was done, and I should have done more to stop it, and for that I truly am sorry." I stared into Penny's eyes, trying to determine what she felt. I couldn't imagine having a granddaughter who was treated the way hers had been, but I couldn't imagine enjoying that experience.

"You didn't make the post?"

"No, ma'am."

"Have you said anything to your *friends* about it?"

"Yes, ma'am. I got them to take it down. Unfortunately, it had been up for more than twenty-four hours, but I did get it removed."

Penny stroked her chin. "I see."

"I have been trying to make it up to Riley. I really do want to clear the air between us, but she has refused to listen to me."

Penny crossed her arms. "Can you blame her?"

"No, ma'am."

"Well, I'm glad to hear you have guilt from the situation. I would prefer that it never happened, but remorse is important in the process." Penny sighed. "I can't guarantee Riley will ever come around. She was hurt by the situation. But, if you do want things to change or be her friend, you'll have to work for it. It won't be easy. My Riley bug is stubborn."

"I understand. Mrs. Br— I mean Penny, can I ask you a question?"

"Okay."

"Why didn't you say something in front of my aunt or Estella?"

Penny smiled. "Why bring more pain into a situation that is already heightened?"

"Well, thank you. Not many people would do that, especially with a Rowe. You could have made fun of me or embarrassed me here."

Penny crossed her arms. "That's not how I work, and I hope that's not how you will anymore either." Penny patted my shoulder and returned to Estella.

How could she be so nice to me when I had been so horrible to her granddaughter? My mother would have shamed them or worse. Was Penny right? Was it better to spread happiness or compassion than pain and embarrassment?

My aunt waited for me by the table. "What was all that about?"

I shook my head. "I'll tell you in the car."

Delilah shrugged and walked side by side with me to her rental. How would I explain what had happened? And better yet, did I want my aunt to know how awful I had been to someone else? I wasn't so sure.

e walked through the back door of my parent's house, laughing. After I told my aunt what had happened with Penny, she had been really understanding about the situation.

I set my clutch purse on the table. "Now you, worst memory from high school."

She touched her chin then smirked. "Someone threw up on me at the homecoming football game."

I scrunched my nose. "Oh, gross!"

"Oh yeah. It dripped down my back and was in my hair. It was super."

"Ew. I don't know how I would have survived that at all. You must have been—" I froze at the sound of heels clacking against the floor. It could only be one person, and from the sound of it, she was livid.

Sure enough, within seconds, my mother flung open the doors and glared between the both of us. "Where *have* you been?"

"We—"

She raised her hand to cut me off. "I don't actually care where you've been. What I care about is that you *blew off* Luke at the stables today and have been out all afternoon. It's seven o'clock! You missed hours' worth of ball preparations. We can't get that time back. Not to mention, do you want to completely derail everything your father and I have done for this family name? The Warringtons won't be around forever, and, if you screw this up with Luke, you will never do anything again."

Delilah moved closer to my mother. "Vivi, come on. Take it easy. She saw that boy at the stables. He was rude, if you ask me, and then we went to play pinochle."

I cringed.

My mother's face reddened. "*Pinochle!* You skipped out on

your duties to play cards? Have you forgotten everything? I knew Delilah coming here would cause a mess for you. We're at such a crucial place, if you two screw this up"—she fanned her face—"I won't forgive either of you. No more ditching the schedule. Do you understand me?"

I stood there silent and stunned. I didn't know how to respond. Of course, I knew she wanted me to say yes, but, in a matter of seconds, she had cut me down and ripped me to shreds and didn't bother caring about a word of it.

"Of course, Mother. I'm sorry. I should have known better. It won't happen again. You have my word."

"No way. Shelby, do not apologize. You haven't done anything wrong. Vivian, do you hear yourself? You're being absolutely ridiculous! She had an afternoon with her aunt. She went on that forced horse ride and obliged the encounter. She's a seventeen-year-old girl; she should have the freedom to do things she wants."

Vivian squared her shoulders with Delilah. "She should apologize. She was insubordinate today. She knew her schedule was booked, and yet, she went off with you instead of keeping her plans with Luke. This needs to go off without a hitch. He is from a prominent family, and she will do good to keep him on the line."

"Keep him on the line? Are you crazy? This isn't the eighteenth century. Women can pick their own dates and relationships. You aren't seriously contemplating arranging who she can be with, are you?"

Vivian crossed her arms. "I certainly am. Shelby is a *Rowe*. She has obligations to uphold. She doesn't get to be some silly, high school lovestruck teenager."

What was happening? Were they really arguing about my life as if I wasn't here? And did my mother really think so little of me that she would rather choose than let me have the sense to do it myself? If names were all they valued instead of substance, this whole ordeal would be excruciating. Luke was a barbarian, even with his private preppy upbringing. He may know general etiquette, but he didn't know how to be a genuine gentleman.

Delilah threw up her arms. "It's not about being silly! She has rights, Vivian. Do you really want to put her in a relationship with someone for their name?"

"What's wrong with being in a relationship with a prominent family?"

"Do you hear yourself? A name is just that—a name! Don't you want to make sure the boy will treat your *only* daughter with respect and dignity?"

"He's a Warrington; that's all he will do."

Delilah huffed. "Oh sure, I forgot. Because he is from a well-to-do family, he is gifted with genuine characteristics of kindness, generosity, respect, and integrity. It happens like magic, all from a name."

"Names are important, Delilah. You of all people should know that."

Delilah faked smacking herself in the head. "Oh, I forgot! I'm a Bryant, nothing more. I was in a delusion that I had a sister who was born a *Bryant* too. Maybe I imagined her, because she sure seems dead."

I gasped. The fight intensified, and I couldn't listen to them fight over me anymore. I turned on my heels and snuck from the room. I walked aimlessly in the hallway, trying to figure out where I would go. This wasn't how I wanted to end my evening with my aunt. I had hoped for takeout and a fun movie. Instead, they decided to fight over my life and not ask what I thought. I didn't know what was worse: the things my mother said about me or the fact no one thought to ask what I wanted. How did I have such a powerful name but stripped of all freedom to do anything or say anything I wanted to?

I entered the foyer and stared at the Christmas tree between the two grand staircases. It was chock full of ornaments that someone else had placed there. Not a single one was handmade or sentimental; my mother had bought them from a catalog to make the home feel cheery and joyful. When instead, I felt empty and sad as I stared into it. All I longed for was a true Christmas with my parents and aunt—one where we shared stories and laughter, not trivial schedules decided by other people.

I would even settle for decorating a tree or watching a few holiday movies together at this point. I shook my head. That was impossible. I knew how my mother and father were. It would never happen, no matter how hard I wished for it.

The shouting emanated from the kitchen. I covered my ears and pressed hard until the shouting dissipated. This wasn't how anything should have happened.

I longed for a different reality, one where being me was acceptable. I didn't want to be told anymore Rowe-etiquette rules. I wanted to be my own person, but tonight showed me that would be impossible. There was no way I could be myself and not disappoint my mother.

I recalled what Penny had told me earlier. She had wondered why someone should add pain to a heightened situation. What she didn't understand was that was all I ever saw. No one ever spread kindness in the Rowe household. It was about image, nothing more. What would I give to have a family like Riley had? Penny would never diminish who Riley was for family gain. She wouldn't force her to be with someone ingenuine. No one understood why I wanted to be her friend, but she was the only person who would never know the family obligations I carried every day. That freedom was envious, and, if I could only hold on to a little bit, I could be me.

CHAPTER 7

J awoke the next morning feeling hungover from the emotional baggage of my mother and my aunt's fight. What had they been thinking to argue like that in front of me? Didn't they realize I could defend myself—or better yet, I could make my own decisions for the betterment of the family? Maybe if they trusted me more, I wouldn't find ways to ignore their dogma.

I threw off the covers and stretched. Today would be a longer day of ball prep and hopefully solidifying some ideas for the proposal to the founding family council. Still rubbing my eyes, I walked to my bathroom. I smacked my cheeks a couple times and stared into the mirror. I would rather sleep or binge watch shows online all day. Most of my classmates got to use this time to do whatever they wanted. I, on the other hand, had to continue to promote my families' name.

I turned on the shower and gathered my towels and clothes. If I was late to breakfast, things would be worse. I showered quickly, towel wrapped my hair and dressed in a long red tunic and black leggings. Red would pop my blue eyes, and it brightened my complexion with my dark brown hair. I settled for my black riding boots that went high on my calves, and now it was time for makeup. Oh, how I envied people who could go to breakfast in their PJs. But my mother expected me to look beautiful at any time. I could only relax in my room, nowhere else.

I searched for my foundation as her voice chimed in my head, *"We always dress for company, Shelby. You never want to be caught by others in sweatpants."*

If I ever had a family, I wouldn't care what they wore, as long as they were happy.

I settled on a more natural look for my makeup then put away everything. Taking one last look at my reflection, I headed for the lion's den.

I took the back stairs one by one as I strained to hear any noise from the kitchen or dining room. If anyone had been talking, they used hushed tones, because I couldn't hear anything. And, if there was one thing about having a huge house with modern decorations, it was the thing echoed like crazy.

I took a deep breath and strolled into the dining room. My mother sat at one end, staring at a magazine, entranced in its pages. She didn't even look up when I entered.

At the other end sat my aunt who continued to scroll on her phone and sip something from a mug. If my nose accurately recognized the smell, it was apple cinnamon cappuccino. We kept it in the cupboard for holidays only.

Of course, I would be welcomed with silence. I sighed as I pulled out a chair and sat. The chair rested perfectly in the middle between them both just in case anyone accused me of taking sides.

I cleared my throat. "Good morning."

Mother glanced up then dropped her gaze to stare at her magazine. "It's about time you joined us for breakfast,

Shelby. If you sleep your day away, you will never accomplish anything."

"Sorry. I'll be more prompt in the future."

"Yes, well, we shall see. Actions are better than words."

I glanced at my aunt who had neglected to stray from her phone. This would certainly be eventful. I grabbed my phone and checked my messages. Nothing new. I scrolled through my contacts until I found Randy's number. I opened a message and typed, *Hey, Randy. Are you free to discuss proposal ideas today?*

The rustling of pages ended, followed by a thud. "Shelby, no phone at the breakfast table!"

"But I need to see if Randy can meet today to discuss the proposal ideas for the founding council."

Mother's eyebrows knitted together, and she pursed her lips. "Why on earth would you be working with that Walker boy?"

I twisted my shirt in my fingers. "Not really working *with* him per se, but I must meet with him at least once."

She tapped her nails on the table. "Where?"

"I don't know. In town somewhere, I suppose."

"Absolutely not. I don't want anyone to see you talking to him. You have him come here, or it doesn't happen at all. Do you understand?"

I nodded. It wouldn't be ideal to meet at the house, but it would be something. We could use the guesthouse so the constant flow of traffic finishing the ball preparations wouldn't bother us.

My phone illuminated to reveal a message. *Yeah, I guess. Does one work? I must finish my shift.*

Sounds good. Meet at my place?

Why don't we meet in town?

Can't. Either my house or I can't meet.

Fine. Be there at one.

My smile faded when I caught my mother's stare. "He'll be here at one."

"You be careful around that boy. His whole family is bad news. I can't believe they are still in the founding family council. What a pity. They bring down all the other families with their behavior."

My bowl of cereal and fruit parfait arrived with Mr. Bennet our butler. I smiled and nodded my thanks. It was impolite to chat with him, otherwise I may distract him from his duties—at least according to my mother.

The parfait had fresh berries and my favorite Greek yogurt. It was in peak freshness. My cereal contained the bland granola and other nuts I had to shovel down. No sugary snacks or cereals for me. However, Chef Frank knew when to sneak me the good stuff. I could always count on him putting something delicious with my granola to help it all go down.

Between bites, I glanced at Delilah. She remained silent and focused on her phone or her food. Had she become upset with me too? I wasn't sure if her silence toward me was because of the overwhelming presence my mother casted in any room or if it was because I had hurt her as well. My attempts at catching her attention had failed too.

The longer I sat, the more I felt like I was a stranger in my own house. The silence was uncomfortable, and I would enjoy having company from someone else, even if my mother didn't approve of the company.

Now I only had to wait for him to arrive.

~

*T*he doorbell rang exactly at one p.m.—or would have if I hadn't been watching out the window to intercept Randy's arrival.

My mother had maintained her brooding silence all day, and I didn't want to subject anyone to that—especially not Randy.

"Right on time."

"Yep. Can I come in?"

"Yes, but not here."

His brow arched in response.

"We are meeting in the guesthouse. It'll be quieter, with less distractions or interruptions."

"You do know this is a business arrangement and nothing else, right?"

"Of course … Oh." My mouth twisted. "I'm not trying to seduce you or anything."

"Mm-hmm. Interesting location choice. It feels like you're hiding me away or something."

"My mother won't let me leave, with all the preparations for the ball."

"Or that's just a nice way of saying your mother doesn't want you seen with me around town."

I gasped. "No. Not at all."

Randy raised his hand. "No point in denying it. I know what the council thinks of my family. I'm here to help change their opinions."

I stared. How could someone be so comfortable with people judging them negatively and yet not have it affect them?

"Shelby, where are we going?"

"Oh, right. This way." I shut the front door and walked around back. The paved walkway to the guesthouse wasn't too long, but it was enough distance from the house to allow some privacy.

The door remained unlocked for guests. Our security system would catch any intruders before they even stepped a toe on the property, not that Honey Cove had many thefts or burglaries. It was too hard to steal from your neighbors when they could name you and your whole family.

We walked through the front door and settled on the couches in the front sitting area.

"Will this work?" I asked.

Randy wiggled on the sofa. "Yeah, it should be fine."

I smiled. "Great. Can I have Mr. Bennet get you anything?"

"No. I'm fine." Randy unloaded several folders and notebooks from his bookbag. "I was thinking Honey Cove should capitalize on its main features."

"Woah, right into it, huh?"

"Yes, that's the point of this whole arrangement, isn't it?"

I nodded.

"Anyway, Honey Cove prides itself on its heritage, its bees, and its cove. So why don't we have functions that draw in crowds to these places? Festivals, carnivals, family nights with scavenger hunts around the town."

I had to admit, for an outcast in the founding family council, Randy had some interesting ideas. "How do you propose we get outside members to join?"

"We partner with certain corporations, and they can send their families here on vacations, for work meetings, you name it."

I stroked my chin. "That could work."

Randy leaned back on the chair. "Well, what are your ideas?"

Crap. In all the arguing and upsets, I hadn't thought about what I would pitch. "I have some tentative plans but wanted to see what you had first."

Randy crossed his arms. "In other words, you were feeling out the competition so you could take credit and leave me in the lurch."

My jaw slackened. "No, not at all."

Randy rubbed the palms of his hands together. "If you didn't plan to actually work with me, why call me here, Shelby? I'm busy. I don't have time for games if you're going to ditch me in the end. I'm sure that's what your father wants anyway."

Nothing would come out of my mouth.

Randy straightened the papers he brought and shoved them in his bag. "That's what I thought. I'll see myself out."

"Wait. Don't go. You're not wrong that I am supposed to do this on my own, but I don't want that. I want to work with you, and I think you have some good ideas. I hadn't developed much on my own, but I would like to if you gave me a chance."

Randy looked apprehensive as his hand froze from putting in the last of what he brought in his book bag. "And you aren't going to take everything and run with it, *alone*?"

"No. I promise."

Randy snorted. "How can I trust you, Shelby?"

I sighed. "I guess you have to take my word for it that I won't cut you out of the deal."

"That's a large leap of faith."

"I know I don't deserve it. You have every right to believe otherwise, but I am trying to be a different person, Randy." I took a deep breath. How many times had I said something like this recently? How many times had I resorted to begging people to believe my word? When had my word become useless in the circles that mattered to me?

"I'll trust you this once. But, Shelby, please don't make me regret it. I don't want other people to be right about who you are."

I smiled. "I won't let you down."

His smile returned, and he set the papers on the table between us.

I perused the research he had done. This was more than I

had planned to even do. Maybe he deserved more credit than I did. More importantly, how would I convince my father to include his name on the proposal? This proved a problem I would need to fix before we pitched at the next meeting.

Randy carefully shared each of his ideas with me, and I beamed. I had convinced him to trust me; I only hoped I was worthy of that trust.

CHAPTER 8

My cheeks ached from the laughing. I enjoyed every minute Randy and I spent working on this project. He hesitated at first to trust me, but when he finally let go and allowed me to see what he thought, we worked splendidly together.

"I don't think I've laughed this hard in practically forever," I said.

Randy smiled. "Me neither."

It was nice to spend quality time with another human. Randy wasn't using me. He wasn't directing my actions to benefit him or spin something. He pitched ideas for a joint project, no insinuations, no blackmail. "Thank you for trusting me."

"I know you're a good person in there somewhere, Shelby. I've seen it. I just don't know why you let other people wreck it."

I sighed. "You know how the pressure works. This town is insufferable with their expectations."

Randy arched his brow. "This town? Or your parents?"

"Both. When people hear *Rowe*, they expect me to be the

best, be different, to be a debutant. My parents, well, they're far worse. My father expects me to be the son he didn't have and learn the business at arm's length. My mother expects me to be the belle of the ball and royalty, marry well to continue the legacy. Neither of them listen to me or each other."

"I get the talk, believe me. But, Shelby, at some point, you must make the decision to be who you want to be. No one else will stand up for *you* the way you would. No one else will be as invested."

He had a point. Randy did understand the staring and the looks. I didn't have an alcoholic father, but I had expectations and stories circulated about me, just like Randy did. He had to help his father's company because his dad was unfit to run it anymore. My father refused to fully release control. Instead, he gave me these *projects* to test how well I would uphold the family name. I was sick of it all.

"You're right, I know that. But I can't help wanting to please them. I want them to be proud of me. I want people to be proud of the Rowes, but no one listens to how I want to do it."

"Then make them listen."

"That's easy for you to say."

Randy scoffed. "It wasn't easy and isn't easy to ignore what people say about my family. Your father included. I know what the other founding families think of mine. We are pariahs, holding on by a thread, but I don't let it stop me. You need to make a choice, Shelby. Either you're unhappy in your own life as those around you control your decisions or you do something about it and risk what others will think." He shoved the remaining papers in his bag and stood.

I stared at him, wondering how he had become so wise in the face of adversity. I supposed that was my answer right there, but I didn't know I would have taken the same path had things been the same. I moved closer to Randy to help with his things. I reached to hug him as a gust of winter wind blew through the room and rustled the curtains. "What the …?"

Luke strolled in, haughty as ever. When his gaze fell upon the scene, his smirk became a glare and it aimed right for me.

"Luke, what are you doing here?" I asked.

Luke's eyebrows rose. "What am I doing here? What are *you* doing here?"

I folded my arms. "Last I checked, this was the guesthouse on *my* estate. You, however, don't live here."

"While that may be true, you still shouldn't be here with Walker."

Randy coughed. "Walker is my last name, and Shelby can do as she pleases."

Luke faced me. "You aren't backing out of our deal to go with *him*, are you?"

Randy put his hands in front in self-defense. "Woah. Just because I'm here doesn't mean I'm seeing Shelby. So, whatever arrangement you two have isn't being screwed up on my account. I was working on a project with her, but we're done, so I was leaving."

"Shelby? Is this true?"

I rolled my eyes. "What if it is? We aren't dating. I don't owe you any explanation."

Luke huffed and rammed his hands deeper into his coat pockets. "I disagree. To the world we are very much together, and that means you do owe me an explanation."

Randy strode across the room and stood at the door. "Shelby, I've got to go. See you at the ball."

"See you then." I couldn't blame him. Luke was being insufferable, and, if I was him, I wouldn't stick around either. If it weren't for my mother's *arrangement*, I wouldn't stick around. I huffed and plopped on the couch. "Luke, why are you here?"

"I asked you a question first. What is Walker doing here?"

"As *Randy* said, we had a project to do. Now, why are you here?"

Luke sat on the sofa opposite me and straightened his posture. "I'm here to spend time with you. We must seem coupled and only have one day left until the ball. It's crunch time."

I wrinkled my nose. "Crunch time? We aren't going to be interrogated at this party. I think we'll be fine."

Luke slammed his hand on the couch. "It will *not* be fine, Shelby. People will be looking and listening. You don't think the gossip queens of this town will be watching us? If we can't even manage a decent conversation in private, how do you expect to do it tomorrow night?"

I drew my face into what I liked to call my publicity smile: no crinkles by my eyes, showing all my teeth, and positively radiant. "Because I'll wear this smile, walk side by side with you." I rose and sat near him on the couch, letting my hand hover just by his until we touched slightly. I moved my other arm around to his shoulder and stared into his eyes. "I'll look for you attentively, and when we are apart, I'll look dreadful. And for all those silly bubbleheaded attention seekers, they will believe it—hook, line, and sinker." I watched as Luke shifted uncomfortably and averted his gaze.

"Just like you just did."

I stood and flipped my hair as I sashayed to the door. I knew I could fool everyone into thinking I liked Luke, but I absolutely refused to do it when I didn't have to.

I found my mother in the same place I had left her that morning—at the dining room table. "Mother, why did Luke show up in the guesthouse?"

Without looking up, she plastered a grin across her face. "Ah, so my present found you."

"Present? You call Luke a present?" I squeezed my hands together, my nails digging into my palms. "Why is it so imperative that he spends time with me?"

Mother's gaze snapped up to meet mine. "Because I asked him and *you* to do so. That is all the reason you need."

I crossed my arms. "I was busy working on the proposal for Father. He interrupted our work."

"That Walker boy needed to go home anyway. Why you listened to him for that long is beyond me. Luke is a gentleman. He is my choice for the ball. Did you at least sit with him this time?"

"No, Mother. I can easily *act* like we're together tomorrow night."

"Why is it so difficult for you to follow directions, Shelby?"

"I will follow all of your directions tomorrow night. Your precious ball will go off without a hitch."

Mother's eyes narrowed. "It better, and I don't know why you would resist spending time with someone who has been brought up like you and understands our family."

I turned on my heels and left. My mother was insufferable. Why this arrangement was so important to her I would never understand. How would Luke Warrington help our families so entirely? What could he possibly do for me? Rowes were more important in the community, more connected.

With each stair, I stomped harder. I stalked into my room and slammed the door. Randy was right; no one would fight for me better than me. I had to do something for myself. I wouldn't do it at my mother's ball, but once my obligation for that evening ended, I would do what I could to change. I was done being a puppet for my parents.

I sat on my four-poster bed and sulked. I wanted something fun to do. I wanted true friends to talk to. I wanted someone to confide in. My aunt was off limits. She usually acted as a sounding board, but ever since their argument, things were hazy, and Delilah seemed absent more and more frequently.

My phone vibrated across the nightstand. With nothing else to occupy myself, I checked the message to see Tabitha had texted the group chat. *Shelby, what are the colors for your mom's ball this year? I don't want to clash with any of the decorations.*

Priscilla followed suit with her own text. *And what color is your dress? We don't want to be too matchy-matchy.*

I huffed. What was with them? They tried entirely too hard to make me like them, and, at this point, I didn't know why they bothered. Of course, they wanted to know what colors to wear or not wear, but I didn't care if they blended in with the entire backdrop of the party. It served them right.

I dropped the phone onto the nightstand and laid on my bed. I would force sleep or at least rest. Tomorrow would begin early and end late. I needed as much sleep as I could manage.

CHAPTER 9

$\mathcal{I}$ awoke from the sound of my mother yelling through the speaker in my room. "Shelby Elizabeth Rowe, wake up *this* instant."

I sighed. I knew today would be stressful for my mother, but I hadn't expected to receive such a warm welcome when I awoke.

The covers slanted off my bed and dropped as I walked to the speaker to respond. "I'll be right down."

She never answered, and I didn't waste a second. I threw on jeans and a large day hoodie. It was perfect for this type of occasion, because what was the point of getting fully dressed when I would have to get ready for real later? This was much easier and prevented my mother from freaking out any further for my tardiness.

At the top of the stairs, I could already hear the hustle and bustle down below. Someone shouted at a high decibel, while the clacking of heels on tile reverberated around me. *Oh, joyous.*

The sight from the bottom of the stairs was not much better. People ran back and forth through the foyer from

70

outside into the room for the ball. I could only imagine my mother was making everyone pay for any delay in what she thought it should take.

I scanned the ballroom for my mother and found her surrounded by employees in all black attire all carrying notebooks or paper of some sort.

"How incompetent are you all? I simply asked for the tables to be arranged at this end of the room with eight places at each. Is that so difficult? I need all the flatware, plates, and centerpieces on the tables *yesterday*. Let's go people! Today is the day." Mother held the bridge of her nose between two fingers.

"How can I help, Mother?"

She snapped her attention to me. "Finally. I thought you would sleep the day away. It's bad enough your aunt is missing, your father isn't home, but then my *only* daughter is sleeping away her life." She tapped her foot. "You can go see what is taking these incompetent oafs so long to bring in the centerpieces!" Vivian's voice rose to a shrill pitch by the end of her demands.

I turned quickly and left the room, searching the foyer for the people in charge of centerpieces. It most likely was Christine, the same woman who provided flowers every year. How she tolerated my mother year after screaming year I would never know, but she did.

Christine huddled over a bouquet of white and red roses. Roses and other flowers of red and white hues surrounded her van.

I cleared my throat, hoping not to startle her. "Christine ... I'm sorry to bother you. Can I do anything to help with the centerpieces?"

Christine shifted her weight and stood. "Shelby." She smiled as her gaze settled on my face. "Your mom sent you, didn't she?"

I nodded.

"Okay, how about you grab a few of the votives from my van, choose three different ones and then show them to your mom. When she can choose the votive she likes the best, I can finally narrow down the flowers she wants."

"Okay, no problem."

I walked to the side of the van and opened the door. All along the floor were several votive choices. I scanned the choices and settled on a squat, round one and a tall, slender one and a medium height with delicate patterns on the side. All the votives were gold, to match my mother's theme colors.

I carried the options through the front door and searched for my mother. As far as I could tell, she hadn't moved from the spot I had left her moments before.

Mother caught sight of me before I had stopped in front of her. She took a few loud steps and met me in the middle. She snatched the medium votive with delicate patterns of wispy vines. "This one. I love it. What do you think?"

"I agree."

"Perfect. I need the flowers as soon as possible. Once the tables are ready, we must decorate the windows, banisters, and the entry with flowers."

I hurried back to Christine. The faster I worked, the easier it was for my mother's mood to improve. I held up the chosen votive. "My mother likes this one."

Christine smirked. "I had a feeling she would choose that one. Okay, so I brought several options for her. They are all red and white flowers. Take two roses, two amaryllis, two carnations, two lilies, two gardenias, and two orchids."

I watched carefully as she pointed to each of the bins and grabbed what she asked. I sprinted back to my mother with the handful of flowers.

Vivian was waiting for me at the ballroom entrance. She

snatched the flowers from my hand as soon as I was close enough. "She brought lilies? No, absolutely not. Those things *reek*. Roses are a must, orchids, and let's do the amaryllis. Can you let her know?"

I nodded, but my mother had already turned away and walked toward someone else to verbally abuse.

Christine waited with her hands on her hips.

I had separated the flowers my mother chose in one hand and the ones she didn't want in the other. "This hand she approved and is good to go."

Christine studied each one. "Come back in twenty minutes and I'll have all the centerpieces done perfectly so they can go on the tables."

"Thank you."

"No problem, darlin'. It's my job."

I returned to the ballroom and kept my hands safely tucked behind me. I wasn't sure what my mother would expect me to do next, but I knew it would be nonstop until the room and the foyer were absolutely perfect.

~

A mere two hours later and I was exhausted. Christine had kept her promise, and in twenty minutes, she was done with the centerpieces. An hour later and the windows were completed with red and white poinsettias, and another thirty minutes after that, she had decorated the entrance with flowers.

My mother, however, was unimpressed with the productivity. Personally, I think she frantically paced the room because my father had yet to appear, and only seven hours remained until everyone arrived, let alone the six maximum hours left before he had to get ready. The closer the clock ticked to six, the cruder she became.

"Shelby!" my mother screamed.

I startled. "Yes?"

"Ah, there you are. Make yourself useful and find your Aunt Delilah. I need that *horrendous* rental car to disappear before people start to arrive."

I practically ran from the room. My nerves were on edge. The shrill screams and short responses was enough to send me on high alert. I welcomed the opportunity to find my aunt. I only hoped it took a long time so I could avoid my mother. I knew she wanted things to go well and be perfect, but she really needed to learn how to deal with her anxiety without unleashing it on the world. People could do their job and be efficient without her acting unhinged.

I took the stairs two at a time and took my time as I meandered down the long hallway toward the green room, which sat at the end of the hallway, the farthest from the master bedroom at the complete opposite end. My aunt had hidden for a reason, and I certainly didn't blame her. As far as I could tell, neither of them had apologized or mended fences. I couldn't imagine my mother *ever* apologizing; she was never wrong in her eyes, so how would she end up having to apologize?

I knocked lightly on the green room's large door. I half expected no one to answer, but, within a few seconds, I heard a loud shuffle on the other side, followed by the door widening a few inches.

Delilah peered through the crack. "Oh, Shelby." She widened the opening. "It's you. Come in."

I smiled and sauntered into the room. I plopped on the queen-sized bed and surveyed the state of the room. Clothes draped over the armchairs by the door, and several bags with what I assumed to be makeup sat on the vanity in the bathroom to the right. It was neat for my aunt's style but certainly not as clean as it normally would have been.

Delilah eyed me warily. "So, what does your mother want me to do?" She crossed her arms. "I'm sure it's something so *very* important."

I giggled. "You know her so well. She wants to make sure the rental is invisible tonight from the guests. She would *die* if someone thought it belonged to her."

Delilah's well-manicured eyebrow rose. "Oh, she would, would she? Hmm, if only I had known sooner."

"Aunt Delilah!"

She chuckled. "I'm only kidding, but she could use a forklift to remove the stick shoved up her—"

"Aunt Delilah!"

"Okay, okay. I'm sorry. She just gets under my skin. How has she been today?"

I rolled my eyes. "Top level awful."

"I figured as much."

"Yep, exactly as you would expect. She has sniped at everyone downstairs even if they did what she asked."

Delilah shook her head. "Predictable. Has your father shown up yet?"

"Nope. Not sure where he is, but you can tell it's making her crazy."

"Making her crazy? She's already there."

"True, but she keeps getting worse as the time continues. I was glad she sent me on this errand, because I didn't know how much more I could take of her shrill voice."

"That's why I stayed up here. I'm out of the way. I can't hear a word of her shouting, and she can't blame me later for a decision she ultimately made. If I'm not there, I can't be blamed."

"True, although I doubt that would work for me. It would be my fault if I was there or not."

Delilah outstretched her hand. "Come with me to move

the car. Get some air and then we can come back in and deal with your mother. Together."

It was the best scenario in this situation. It was easier to deal with Mother's idiosyncrasies in teams.

"So, we are still expecting the arrival of that boy tonight, right?"

"Unfortunately."

Delilah pretended to shiver. "I don't like him; something seems off."

"You and me both. I don't have a choice though. Mother is only worried about two founding families making connections. He could be the worst specimen of man on the planet and she would still find a way to accept him."

Delilah grabbed my hand as we walked. "I'm sorry, Shelby. That's not okay. You would think your mother would remember what it was like before her precious last name. She wasn't always like that."

"I can't imagine her any other way."

Aunt Delilah smiled. "She was a lot like you actually."

My eyebrows rose. "Like me? I doubt that."

"No really. She was spirited, stubborn obviously, but she was warmer."

I scrunched my nose. "Warmer? I can't imagine that at all."

Delilah sighed. "Well, when things happen to you, you tend to change."

I crossed my arms. "What happened to her?"

Aunt Delilah shifted from foot to foot. "It's not my place to tell you about your mother when she was younger. She wouldn't want me to."

"So? I can't picture it. For all I know, you could be making it up."

Aunt Delilah nibbled on the bottom of her lip. "Oh alright. But, if you tell her I told you, you're dead meat."

We tiptoed hand in hand down the back stairway into the kitchen. It was highly unlikely my mother would be there, but it was better safe than sorry. If she caught us, she would cause a scene and make us do something else.

"I know you've heard me say that we both used to be Bryants."

I sucked in a deep breath of the cold air. "Yeah?"

"Well, we weren't that well off. Kind of like the Brooks family actually."

"Riley's mom-mom?"

Delilah nodded. "We weren't well known, so we didn't have much baggage, but we weren't founding-family material. Your mother had higher aspirations. She wanted to do something of importance in this town. She wanted to be someone, to make a difference."

How had I not known we had both shared so many ambitions?

"In high school, Thad didn't pay any attention to your mother. I doubt he even realized she existed. He was popular beyond belief. I mean, his family owned the most shares in Honey Cove. It didn't matter what he did; he couldn't be at fault for anything. Your mother didn't like his arrogance, but she respected his position."

Delilah silently unlocked the rental, and we climbed in. She eased the car into Drive and put it at the farthest end of the driveway—almost toward the stables but directly behind the guesthouse. No one would see unless they left the party to explore the grounds—which was forbidden.

We exited the car, and she hit the lock button.

"Your mother didn't set her sights on Thad, but she did have her eye on some other well-to-do boys. Your mother wasn't afraid to go after what she wanted, so she walked up to him and asked him out. The girls hanging around his group laughed their heads off then squared their shoulders at her. They all chanted that she was no good and had no business being around him."

I gasped. "She was turned away? But she has said those exact same words to me about other people. You'd think she wouldn't be like that if it had happened to her."

Aunt Delilah frowned. "I think it affected her in the opposite way. Because she had went through that experience, she was determined to never be embarrassed that way again. I think she took it to the extreme and became what she didn't like about those other people. It would prevent her from looking like a fool."

"So, how did she end up with my father if she wasn't considered good enough?"

"It was after high school, her first year in college. Something had shifted. She had recreated herself and caught his attention." She shrugged. "I don't understand all the parts about their relationship, but I do know that day haunted her. Changed her. She was more focused on what her appearance and stature could do to make changes."

"I had never realized she went through that."

"That's life. You never know what people have going on, but it doesn't excuse how she treats people now. She should know better, but, for whatever reason, she blocks that part out."

"Hmm. Who was the guy?"

Aunt Delilah looked away and toward the house. Her eyes became distant. "I don't remember."

A heavy gust blew between us, and I shivered. I had forgotten that we would have to walk to the house after we parked the car.

"Are you looking forward to tonight?" my aunt asked, changing the subject.

I shrugged. "Yes and no. I'm excited to see certain faces,

but I'm not excited about the arrangement or any of the founding-family obligations."

"That makes sense. You sure get a fair amount of them."

I laughed. "That's putting it lightly. Sometimes I wonder who I would be without them. I can't imagine making choices because that was what I wanted or interested me. I always have to worry about the Rowe name or how it makes us or the company look. It's never about me and always about the image. Even my friends at school are only friends because they are founding families."

Delilah frowned. "You don't have anyone you trust?"

"No. Tabitha and Priscilla hang around me for their own personal gain. Neither one of their dads head things in the council; it's always an uncle or grandfather. Priscilla's family is close, but even then, it would go to her brother, not her."

"Ah, so they escalate themselves through you."

"Mm-hmm. Like with the whole Riley situation. I wanted to be her friend. Truly friends. But those two ruined that when they made that awful post. I've tried to show her that's not who I want to be, but I don't blame her for not wanting to listen to me."

"Did you invite her tonight?"

"Yes, even though Mother said no. I found out she is coming as someone else's date."

"Will you try again tonight?"

"If I get the chance. I have a funny feeling Luke will be near impossible to avoid."

Delilah chuckled. "Want to come up with a safe word? If you're around me, I'll pull you away from him."

"No. If I don't spend the time I'm supposed to with him tonight, Mother will be unhappy with me. I'd rather not be the target of her pent-up rage."

"Good call."

I shuffled my feet and kicked a solitary stone from the pavement. "Did you ever find a dress for tonight?"

"Yes, I did. It's something I've worn before, but that's fine with me."

"I'm sure it'll be beautiful. I always love your taste."

Aunt Delilah wrapped her arm around my shoulder as we walked. "Thanks, Shelby."

We hurried our pace and reentered through the back door in the kitchen. A male's voice floated above the rest as I closed the door. I approached the sound with my aunt in tow. My eyes widened as I surveyed the scene.

My father stood in the foyer with my mother a few feet to his right. Her arms frantically waved around her head then to her sides. Whatever they were discussing, it seemed serious. As I got closer, I caught the end.

"You didn't think to arrive a *tad* sooner?" my mother asked.

My father's eyebrows knitted together. "Vivian, please don't start. I've had a long day."

My mother huffed. "Long day …" She trailed off at the sight of us. She straightened her dress and played with the pearls around her neck. "Ah, finally you two have returned." She stared straight into my eyes. "I assume you both have taken care of that hideous car?"

We nodded as my father took the opportunity to turn on his heels and head up the stairs.

"Thad …" my mother whispered to no one in particular.

I stared at her face. Her makeup was natural but evident. Her mouth was drawn into pursed lips, and her eyes appeared sad. They missed their usual sparkle from when she made speeches. I didn't know what had happened between them, but I couldn't stop from feeling sympathetic. My mother worked hard and deserved to be recognized for her efforts—even when she wasn't the nicest about it.

My mother stared at the stairs for a few moments longer then readjusted her stance to face us. "You two better get ready. I don't want you looking like *that* when guests arrive."

Delilah and I exchanged glances. There was no sense in arguing with her, and quite frankly, the dismissal was an excuse to hide in my room until it was time to greet company. And I needed the alone time.

CHAPTER 10

My closet was the best place to get ready for a ball. In the center of the back wall stood a full-length mirror that went from floor to ceiling. On either side of the mirror, shelves lined the walls for my shoes. On the right side of the closet were my formal dresses, purses, and other accessories. The left side of the closet contained my general everyday apparel and accessories. The center of the room had a chaise lounge in case I wanted to take a nap.

I never actually used the chaise lounge for a nap, but I did use it to sit and relax when I avoided my mother. I grabbed the hunter-green dress from its bag and laid it on the chaise. I plopped my white stilettos on the chaise as well. I strolled to the cabinet that contained my fancy jewelry and settled on a light green pendant with icicle designs around the chain and matching bracelet. I also chose my emerald ring with small white diamonds around the outside of the setting. "Perfect."

Once everything was laid out, I turned on my shower. A quick shower would refresh my hair and my skin, making it easier to apply my products. I set my phone on a music station and blasted Christmas songs through the phone speakers. It was my only chance to prepare for the happiness I would need to emanate.

I sighed with the realization that tonight would be full of obligations and acting as if my life was perfect. When, in reality, it had been four days since my last day at school, and I had received only the two messages from Tabitha and Priscilla. No one asked me how my week was going at home. No one sent me well wishes for the holidays.

I shimmied into the warm water and let the feeling wash over me. When I exited the shower, I had to start playing the part, acting like the Shelby Rowe everyone expected me to be, like the Shelby Rowe whose name was done in perfect calligraphy downstairs as it awaited me to sit for dinner—full of pomp and circumstance.

Stop whining!

What was I doing? Everyone who was anyone would be at my house tonight. They all clamored for an invitation to the ball in honor of *my* family. Why wasn't I soaking this up? Why was I whining about all the obligations I had? It could be worse. My parents could ignore me and have no expectations for their only child. I could even be neglected and left to my own devices with no hope of getting what I wanted. So what, my parents had expectations? Shouldn't I be grateful they cared enough to want me to do something with my life? And they treated me like royalty. I could have anything I wanted; all I had to do was ask and curl my hair around my pretty manicured little finger, and I would get it. Plain and simple.

Girls my age would kill for my position. It was time I acted like it.

I twisted my hair in a loose side braid and pinned it with what felt like a thousand bobby pins. I secured my emerald and white diamond hairclip to further secure the braid and looped the rest of my hair in a tight bun. I snatched out a few ringlets of hair and twirled them around my finger, reinforcing the natural curl of my hair.

It took another thirty minutes to finish my makeup— natural and with light tan eye shadow to pop my eyes and dress. My reflection always startled me at the end of applying my makeup. If it had been up to me, I wouldn't bother with makeup, but, as with most things, it wasn't up to me. Makeup was another way to show the town I was perfect … in every way.

Next was the dress. I trudged to my closet and stared at the beautiful gown. It flowed eloquently and hugged me in all the right places. I truly could admire the craftmanship, but it still was another mask I had to wear. I shimmied into the gown and had secured both shoes when a knock echoed through my room.

"Come in!" I shouted.

I straightened and carefully walked to greet my guest.

My aunt Delilah stood in the center of the room, her hand clasped over her mouth. "You look stunning, Shelby."

I beamed. It was always a true compliment from my aunt. Anyone else angled for their own benefit or with their own motives. I stared at the strapless red velvet dress my aunt had chosen. She wore strappy heels with a closed toe. "You don't look bad yourself."

She winked. "Shall we descend into the madness?"

I moved forward and linked my arm with hers. "We shall."

I smiled as we carefully strutted across the hardwood floors into the long hallway and toward the grand staircase.

"It was nice knowing you before I'm fed to the sharks."

Delilah giggled. "It won't be quite that bad."

"Oh, you underestimate those councilmen. They are every bit sharks out for blood."

"I don't envy you tonight. Well, besides that figure and your dress! Seriously, gorgeous."

"Thanks, Aunt Delilah."

"Anytime."

My mother and father waited at the bottom of the stairs. When my mother spotted me, she made a beeline straight for us. Vivian scrunched her nose and eyebrows. "I worried you both wouldn't show. Cutting it down to the last minute." Mother tugged at the tendrils of hair by my temple and finished primping me as I stood motionless.

I resisted the urge to run or tell her I didn't need her help, but that wouldn't help my cause.

"Vivi, you should really work on frowning less. You don't want those forehead wrinkles to become permanent. It costs a lot of money to fix those, yanno."

My eyes rounded as I watched my mother's reaction.

She started to respond then thought better of it. She immediately smiled politely and, through gritted teeth, retorted, "Beautiful dress, Delilah. Hopefully, no one would copy it." She faked a laugh. "What am I saying? It isn't couture, so of course, no one will have it."

Delilah rolled her eyes and chased down a waiter. Guests weren't even here, and the drinking already had begun.

My father joined us. "Shelby, how radiant you look tonight." He lowered his head to whisper in my ear. "Make sure to stay on your best behavior tonight. I have many important men from the council to introduce you and your date to formally. This is an important evening for us."

"Of course, Father."

He nodded and straightened.

My mother smiled and leaned toward him as she whispered in his ear. It didn't last long until my father raised his hand then trailed off in the same direction Delilah had gone.

Since his close arrival, everyone was on edge more than

normal, and I hated it. Why did evenings like this have to cause such strife?

The doorbell rang. As if out of thin air, several butlers approached the door and manned their post by the side. Some had their hands free, while others carried trays with champagne or sparkling cider.

My mother shooed me away from the doors. "To your place in the ballroom, Shelby. A proper Rowe lady wouldn't be caught dead waiting for her guests at the door. Let's not dawdle."

My *place* in the ballroom referred to a spot by a Christmas tree. The lights were supposed to make me seem more jovial and younger, which was ludicrous, but no one asked me. My secondary position was sitting at the table with my name card. No exceptions, ever.

I took a stance by the tree in the far corner. It was the best view to our back yard that sparkled with twinkle lights and an outdoor tree just for this reason. None of us actually went outside to use the tree, and the servants would disassemble it after the ball. But my parents, especially my mother, spared no expense when it came to this blasted thing.

Every southern belle dreamed of a beautiful evening to flaunt a dress and be the center of attention, but it was only girls who had never been in the true eye of everyone who had that dream. I, on the other hand, had been in too many people's eyes to ever wish for it myself. It was a fool's dream.

Guests quickly paraded into the ballroom and scattered toward all the beautiful decorations.

I arranged myself on the side of the tree just out of eyesight, unless one stood at the perfect angle. It had worked until the familiar whiff of cologne invaded my senses.

I coughed. "Luke, can't you go easy with that stuff? I don't need to be drowned in it for people to know we are together tonight."

Luke stared but remained silent.

"What's with you?"

"You … I." He cleared his throat. "You look stunning, Shelby."

I rolled my eyes. "Don't be so flattering when no one can hear you. Save the compliments for our audience."

"I'm not saying it to flatter you. I'm saying it because it's the truth. You're stunningly beautiful."

"Right." I opened my clutch and squeezed my cell from its clutches. It was exactly six o'clock; everyone was right on schedule. I shimmied the phone back into the clutch.

Luke proffered his arm.

I took his arm and surveyed the room. At least he pretended to be a gentleman well. If only he could be a true gentleman all the time instead of his crude, selfish, and egotistical self. What someone would ever see in him was beyond me.

Most of the guests so far were from my father's company. It wasn't until Priscilla and Tabitha arrived that anyone younger was at the ball.

I eyed them both from afar. Despite my silence, they had chosen appropriate gowns that wouldn't make them clash with the décor. Tabitha wore a deep red sequined gown and black Louboutin's. Priscilla went more upscale with embellished ivory crystal heels and a glittery black off-the-shoulder dress. It had a beautiful sweetheart neckline and mermaid bottom. It was stunning, even for Priscilla.

Luke watched me as I eyed Priscilla and Tabitha from across the room. "Don't panic, Shelby. You're by far the most beautiful one in this ballroom tonight."

"Thanks, Luke, but I'm not worried about what anyone else looks like."

He nodded and smiled, but it didn't quite make it to his eyes.

I probably wouldn't have believed me either. I wasn't fully lying, just wasn't the entire truth. Priscilla had a chance to outdo me; it was just her insecurities that came back for her. If she had more confidence, people wouldn't hate her as much for the nasty things she always inflicted on others. Although, I supposed someone else could say similar things to me. I certainly hadn't always been the nicest one around. I had done plenty of cruel things, things I still was ashamed of, but I tried to change. That had to account for something, right?

Priscilla and Tabitha spotted me and strutted my way.

Luke tightened his grip around my arm and into his chest. Did he think I needed protecting?

Tabitha leaned forward to air-kiss my cheek. "Shelby, darling. You look fabulous."

I reciprocated the gesture. "As do you. This color is stunning on you."

She smiled and swished her dress against her ankles.

Priscilla's eyebrow arched as she came closer for a hug. "Beautiful accessories, Shelby. It all really makes your eyes pop."

I strained to smile, knowing anything they uttered about my appearance was merely a nod to social etiquette. It wasn't genuine, at least not in the way I longed for a true compliment.

"Your mother outdid herself this year, Shelby," Tabitha said.

"I'll let her know you think so."

Luke cleared his throat and nudged my side with his elbow.

"Sorry, ladies, how rude of me. You know Luke, obviously, but he's my date."

Luke grinned from ear to ear. "Ladies, you both look radiant this evening."

They both curtsied.

"Well, we would love to stay and chat all night, but we must socialize with the guests. I'll see you two later."

I pulled Luke to stand at the second Christmas tree halfway between both exits.

Luke's eyebrow rose. "Why did we walk away from them? We should be mingling with everyone."

I snorted. "Please, Luke. I will *mingle* with the people who matter. Those two don't matter. They will just gossip about anything they hear anyway, not worth our time."

"Then who should we talk to, in your opinion? I think they matter to everyone else. If you aren't flaunting me to your friends, what will people say?"

"They will have plenty to say, and we can discuss things with them when we are *stuck* at a table for dinner."

"I suppose." Luke moved his arm around me and hovered his right hand on the small of my back.

I bit the corner of my lip to avoid from shivering—or worse, cringing at his touch. It wasn't awful, but it was more than I wish I had to endure.

"You know, you never told me if I looked dashing or not," Luke said with a devilish grin.

I smiled. "You and I both know you do, especially with all of your matchy-matchy to my dress color."

Luke feigned shock. "Is that a compliment from Shelby Rowe. Oh man. Alert Santa we'll have a blizzard."

I rolled my eyes. "Dramatic much?"

"Not at all. I only seem to get snarkiness from you."

I shrugged. "Not always."

"I apologize. You're correct. I get snarky Shelby unless we're pretending to be together. In which case, I get hushed-tone snarky Shelby."

I giggled. "Is that so? How does one emanate snark in a hushed-tone kind of way?"

"I think you know how."

I smiled and looked into his hazel eyes. Okay, so he could be charming when he wanted to.

"There it is."

"There's what?"

"A genuine smile."

My father, with my mother in tow, strutted toward us. "Shelby and Luke, how splendid. You both look exquisite," my father said. "Are you ready to meet a few people, Shelby?"

I followed my parents as Luke accompanied me. I straightened my frame and plastered a smile on my face. It was showtime.

An older couple stood to the side of the ballroom.

My father shook the older man's hand and clapped his back. "Mr. Wyatt, this is my daughter Shelby and her date, Luke Warrington. Shelby, Mr. Wyatt is the head of sales at Rowe Industries."

I curtsied as Luke shook the man's hand.

"It's nice to meet you, Mr. Wyatt," I said.

"Hello again, sir," Luke added.

My mother looked between us all but stayed silent. Her voice echoed in my head, *"A true Rowe woman is seen but not heard. She makes her presence known but never overshadows the man she is with."* I stared at her and longed to know what she actually felt inside. She maintained the wall around so many people that I was unsure if she even knew anymore. She embodied a Rowe woman alright, but I wished I had known her before. Had Delilah been right? Was she still haunted by that memory that she swore to change, even if it changed who she was?

I snuck sideways glances at the rest of the room. It wasn't obvious to either of my parents or I would have been given a death glare, but I was bored with the introductions. By the fourth couple I had met, I lost track of the conversations. I knew their names, because I had been taught names from an early age just for these occasions, but I didn't care if I was being honest.

The crowd parted at the front double doors, and a young couple entered. From the distance, I couldn't decipher the girl, but the closer they came, I realized it was Randy and Riley.

Wow, did they look good together. I watched as Riley held Randy's hands and stared into his gaze. They were so cute together, even if they weren't *dating*, dating. I figured it had to have been Randy's doing, because Riley doted on him to the point where it made no sense that they weren't officially together.

Randy and Riley matched with their candy-apple-red color scheme. Her dress kissed the floor—nothing high end or couture, certainly, but it was perfect for her figure. It was a great color on them both.

I scanned the crowd for Tabitha and Priscilla. I wanted to witness the moment they saw Riley enter. They both huddled by the sparkling cider table with mini quiches. The exact moment they saw her, Tabitha's gaze narrowed, and Priscilla nearly dropped her glass of sparkling cider. I smirked; that had been exactly the reaction I hoped for. Now all I had to do was wait until my mother saw her. I wasn't sure which would be a better scene.

CHAPTER 11

My mother's reaction didn't disappoint. She had seen Randy's date shortly after Tabitha and Priscilla and had a similar reaction, only hers was much more subtle. As her daughter, however, I knew she was unhappy.

Good, let her squirm and think I disobeyed her.

It was almost time to take our seats for dinner. Other than the fact my stomach gurgled like a hungry mountain lion, I didn't take comfort in being stuck at a table with Tabitha, Priscilla, Luke, Randy, and Riley.

Riley glared at me from across the room. I could only imagine how she would feel when she realized we would all sit together for dinner. Luke had slightly redeemed himself. During introductions, he found ways to discuss me and invite me into the conversation, something he certainly didn't have to do. He could have hogged all the attention and no one would have been unhappy with him. As my mother always told me, that was my job as the date anyway. Before me, no female was even close to being in a top position for Rowe Industries or on the founding-families council.

My mother grabbed the microphone and waited as the buzz of conversations settled. "Good evening, everyone. I hope you have all figured out where your seats are for dinner. We will begin dinner momentarily."

"You ready to sit?" Luke asked.

"As ready as I'll ever be," I muttered.

"We could dawdle if you want?"

I shook my head. "Wouldn't look right if a Rowe didn't follow orders."

"You sure?"

"I'm sure I don't want to irritate my mother on purpose. I promised to be good tonight."

We were the first seated, but only for a few moments before Tabitha and Priscilla took their seats to the left of me. Randy would be next to Luke, followed by Riley, which only said Walker plus one on her name card.

Priscilla leaned toward me and whispered, "I *can't* believe Randy invited *her* here! What was he thinking? This is not the place for her."

I leaned away. "Priscilla, don't start. I'm not interested in your petty grudges."

Priscilla's eyes rounded, and Tabitha smirked behind her napkin as she dotted her face with it.

Luke stared intently into his glass of water. *Smart man.* He knew better than to say anything about it.

Randy and Riley appeared at our table, beaming, until they settled on their name cards and the rest of us at the table. I watched as Riley's smile faltered, then she plastered a new but less genuine one on her face.

Randy pulled out her chair and whispered into her ear, causing her to blush before she sat. Once she was seated, he took his place next to her.

Luke watched Randy then leaned toward him. "Hey, man.

I'm sorry about before. I was worried you would steal my girl."

I rolled my eyes. How did he think I was his girl?

Randy nodded and smiled. "No worries. How are you?"

"Enjoying Christmas break until I have to go back."

"Don't get much time before you're shipped away again, do you?" Randy leaned back in his chair. "Have you met my date, Riley, before?"

Riley's cheeks reddened.

Luke reached across the table and shook her hand. "I don't think I have. It's nice to meet you, Riley."

"It's n-nice to meet you too," Riley said.

Tabitha and Priscilla snickered. I lifted the tablecloth and found Priscilla's shin. I kicked her square in the center of her right leg and smiled when she pretended to cough and rub her leg.

She glared toward me, and I turned in response—served her right. I would never understand why she was so adamant about destroying Riley's reputation and social standing. Who cared if she was from New York? Who cared if she wasn't from an upper-echelon family—well, at least the ones she talked to? It shouldn't matter to anyone.

Randy reached across the table for her hand and squeezed. It was so cute it made my heart hurt. He was there for her in a way I never could imagine having myself.

"How's everyone enjoying the ball?" I asked.

"Oh, it's so magical, Shelby. Your mom outdoes herself every year," Priscilla said.

"Can't imagine how she will top this," Tabitha said.

Riley and Randy remained silent.

I leaned toward them. "What do you think?"

Randy met my gaze. "It's beautiful."

Riley raised her glass in agreement.

Hmmph. This wasn't going how I hoped. I thought maybe

all of us being together at a table would help break the ice from the fall, but I should have known that as long as Priscilla and Tabitha were around, Riley would never open up to me. I had to get her alone before she left to apologize. There was no other way around it.

Priscilla slid her finger around the top of her glass, over and over. "So, Riley …" She paused as she let Riley's name hang there.

Riley's gaze darted between us all.

Randy's jaw tightened.

I glared at Priscilla, daring her to act up. I would end the whole thing in seconds. I would never let them get away with their cruelty again.

"Yes?" Riley asked as she stared down Priscilla herself.

"What do you think of the weather here for December? I'm sure it's different than what you would get in New York."

I released the breath I was holding. She had stayed on safe topics … for now.

"It's pleasant. I could definitely get used to the temperature. By now, I would need gloves, scarves, and a hat for my walk to the subway."

Tabitha scrunched her nose. "You took the subway?"

"Why wouldn't she? It's the main form of transportation. What do you think she'd do, drive or take a taxi to school every day?" I asked.

Priscilla shrugged. "She could have a driver …"

I glared at Priscilla, daring her to finish that sentence.

"We all know my family didn't have the money for a driver, Priscilla. If you want to make fun of my wealth, get it over with. I won't wait on bated breath all night until you pounce on something."

Randy smirked and eased back in his chair.

Luke's eyes rounded. "Ladies, there's no need for any of

that, is there? We're here for a celebration and to have a fun evening. Must we discuss the wealth of our *parents?*"

"N-no. We don't," Priscilla stammered.

"Good." I raised my water glass to the rest of the table. Slowly, everyone followed suit. "Let's have a toast to a splendid Christmas season and good tidings to all."

We clinked glasses. "Cheers."

Everyone at the table sipped their glasses as the waiters brought forth the first course—green tomatoes with pistachio relish. I stared at my plate and felt my mouth water. This had always been one of my favorite courses my mother used. She rotated her menu, so it was never the *exact* same for any year.

We sat in silence as we ate. It wasn't until Tabitha finished her plate that anyone spoke.

"Shelby, how long have you and Luke been *dating?*"

I nearly choked on my bite. This was a trap, one I hadn't expected to have asked so directly. For Tabitha to ask the question out in the open wasn't her normal strategy. They were more subtle than this.

"It's a new relationship," Luke answered and rested his hand over mine.

Tabitha leaned forward. "Must be, because I've never heard anything of it. Have you Priscilla?"

Priscilla pursed her lips. "Not at all, Tabitha."

Riley rolled her eyes from across the table.

Randy shifted away.

"Yes, well, Shelby and I have always been intrigued by each other. This is the first time I've been single in a while, and when I saw her at the barn the other day, I knew I had to get to know her better." He stared into my eyes in a warm and endearing way. "The way her hair fell over her shoulders and how her blue eyes sparkle when she's on a mission hooked me." He leaned back and patted his mouth with his napkin. "Did you know she can ride a horse? I mean, like really ride? She practically galloped with Rio the whole ride. She's a woman of many talents."

He remembered the name of my horse? I had ditched him the whole time, and he remembered details like that? I shook my head. What was I saying? What was I doing? He remembered because he had to. I couldn't think he was on my side; that would be dangerous.

Priscilla rolled her eyes. "Some story. You two aren't really together, are you?"

I clasped my other hand over his. "Of course, we are, Priscilla. How could you say otherwise?"

Tabitha's eyebrows knitted. "You two *barely* touch all night or talk, and we're expected to believe this is genuine?"

"Believe what you want, but we know how we feel about each other," Luke said.

I had to admit it; he sold his side of the story well. If I hadn't known any better, I would have believed him too.

"Who cares? Shelby's business is her own. Don't be so jealous that you have to try to embarrass her in front of everyone," Randy interjected.

Riley pulled at his arm sleeve. I couldn't blame her. Why would he stick up for me when he didn't have to? I could handle it, and now they would target him.

Priscilla's glare narrowed. "We don't enjoy being fed lies, Randy. That's why we care. Why do you care to protect her? Don't you have your own hands full with the drama that your *date* causes?"

Riley's jaw slackened, then she quickly recovered. "Why—"

I stared them both down. "Enough, you two. Honestly, this is a dinner party. Do you two need reminders about your etiquette? I hardly think your *parents* would want to hear of your passive-aggressive behavior at this dinner party. Do you?"

Priscilla crossed her arms, and Tabitha scowled. That should end that nonsense for now. The wait staff cleared our plates as the second course arrived. I had to be honest; I was ready for the distraction. This dinner already had me on edge, and it wasn't even halfway over. This would be a long evening.

~

I had never been more excited to get up from a dinner table than tonight. Some comments continued, but it was more of the tension-filled atmosphere that unnerved me the most. Riley exchanged glares with Tabitha and Priscilla when it spiked, but Randy would calm her down.

After the staff had served dessert then cleaned up, I bolted from the table, happy to be anywhere but stranded with all of them. The tension was more than I could handle.

Luke followed by my side as I took a breath in the foyer. "That was intense."

"You're telling me."

"Aren't they your friends? You all go to the same high school, right?"

I shrugged. "Depends how you define the word *friend*, I suppose."

Luke scrunched his nose. "What does that mean?"

"It's nothing. Yes, I see Priscilla and Tabitha every day at school."

"They didn't seem friendly, considering."

"Not their style. I figured they would have something to say ... about all things that transpired." I twirled the strap of my clutch around my finger. "About what you said earlier, how did you remember my horse's name?"

He chuckled. "I pay attention, Shelby. I walked around the stables several times while I waited for you to show up. I stared at his nameplate every time I walked by." He shrugged. "Details like that stay with me."

"Oh."

"I meant what I said though. You are one good horse rider. It's a shame you don't do competitions or something."

I snorted. "A Rowe should be prim and proper, not chasing animals around a ring."

Luke slouched. "You want to do it, don't you?"

"Yeah, but it's another one of those things not allowed by a Rowe woman. It is what it is."

"Shall we get back into the ball? I'm sure they're opening dancing up soon."

I smiled. "You go ahead. I'll be there in a moment."

"Okay, just hurry back. I don't want anyone to talk."

I waved off Luke. He meant well, I supposed, but I still needed some privacy. I walked to the back part of the staircase and sat on the bench. It was out of view from most people and was the perfect place to hide on these kinds of occasions.

The sound of heels echoed across the tile floor, and I cringed.

Please don't be my mother. Please don't be my mother.

My request had been heard, because instead, I saw the familiar candy-apple color I had sat near at dinner. I stood and walked to make my presence known. "Hey, Riley."

Riley spun around. "Oh, I didn't see you there. I just …"

"Needed air?"

"How did you know?"

I gestured to the bench. "I needed the same."

"Oh."

"No worries. I'll keep your secret safe. I'm sorry about Priscilla and Tabitha."

Riley sighed and backed away. "Please don't, Shelby."

I walked forward, meeting her halfway. "I won't try to explain. I just want you to know how awful I feel about everything."

"I know you do."

"But it's not enough?"

"It's not that it isn't enough or that I don't believe your apology. I think you do feel bad. I just don't know that you understand your entire part in the whole mess. I also don't want to open myself up to anything like that again. Things are settling for me here, and I want to keep it that way."

"I understand. I do want to make it up to you."

Riley half smiled. "I don't need it made up to me. It's not about me. It's about you. You should change for you. You'd be happier than having that negative energy around."

"I want to change, but … it's so complicated."

"It's only complicated if you make it complicated, Shelby."

I shrugged.

"I'm going to get back to Randy. I'll see you at school."

"Bye, Riley."

Riley waved and returned through the door. I watched as she sauntered back but froze when I saw my mother staring at me through the opened doors.

Well, crap.

This night went from bad to worse with just a glance.

CHAPTER 12

In my head, my mother's eyes turned red and flames flew from her fingertips. Okay, I guess that wasn't true, but she was angry; that much was clear.

"Shelby!" my mother screamed in a hushed whisper. "What are you doing out here? And why are you with her? Speaking of, how did that little miscreant get on the guestlist? I told you no."

I crossed my arms. "Hello to you too, Mother. I was talking to her after my dinner table had some rude comments thrown her way. I was apologizing on behalf of the Rowes. You know, you wouldn't want someone running away from *our* ball in tears, would you?"

Her eyebrows knitted together. "No."

"Exactly. And I didn't invite her; she was Randy's plus-one. Maybe you should check your own guestlist before you blame me." I stomped into the ballroom.

She called after me. "Don't think we're done talking, young lady."

I rolled my eyes. Of course, she didn't think we were done talking. I'm sure I would even deal with it when everyone went home, but there was still a party to get back to, and until that officially was over, I would make sure to be seen with my date.

Luke was easy to spot. He hadn't made it much farther from our dinner table. He was poised in a conversation with someone I didn't know well.

I nudged his elbow gently with mine once I was next to him.

Luke nodded, showing he acknowledged my presence. At the next opportunity, he introduced me. "Paul, this is my date, Shelby. Shelby, this is Paul, my friend from school."

Paul had blond hair and honey-colored eyes. Even in the dead of winter, his skin was tanned. He either spent a *lot* of time in the sun during the summer or he constantly went to the beach no matter the time of the year.

Paul grasped my hand and kissed the top of it. "Nice to meet a stunning beauty such as yourself."

I blushed. "Thank you. I must admit, I've never seen you around before, Paul. What brings you to Honey Cove?"

"Guilty. This is my first time here. Luke told me I simply couldn't miss it."

"He did, did he?"

"I stay at school during the holiday seasons most of the year. The Warringtons said I could stay a few days and absolutely had to come to the Christmas ball."

"Oh, where are you from?"

"Georgia, but I'm rarely ever there anymore."

"Do you like your school?"

Paul chuckled. "Does anyone ever like their high school?"

I laughed. "True, although I don't mind Honey Cove High."

Paul feigned shock. "What? A high schooler who likes high school? What is this madness?"

Luke smiled.

"Yep, that's me."

Paul eyed the crowd. "Well, I don't want to dominate too much of your time. It was nice to meet you, Shelby." He tapped Luke's arm. "See you at school."

Luke waved as he walked away then faced me. "You two seemed to get along well."

I laughed. "I can be friendly when I want."

"Ah, I see. So, you don't want to be my friend then."

My cheeks reddened. "I'm sorry. I should apologize. I don't mean to be awful to you. I just hate being told what to do and how I should be."

"I understand. This wasn't my idea either, but I'm not the big bad wolf."

"Duly noted." I had forgotten his parents had probably asked him to be my date too. Had I been so naïve that he had been in this deal for all the wrong reasons? Was it possible he was just doing what he was told too?

I pinched the inside of my hand. "Let's dance." I cleared my throat. "It'll look good to the gossipers."

He guided us to the center of the ballroom. The tables had been moved to the side or removed completely to make a large dancefloor. The speakers started with traditional Christmas songs and moved into a slow instrumental dance number.

He grabbed my hands and placed them on his shoulders as he rested his hands above my waist. His placement wasn't too low or too high but perfectly centered.

I looked up into his gaze.

He stared at me intently.

"What?" I asked.

"Nothing. You're breathtaking."

I looked at our feet. "Thanks."

He lifted my chin to meet his gaze. "You're welcome. I

mean it, you know? I'm not just saying it to butter you up. I hope you know that."

I nodded.

"Shelby?"

"Hmm?"

"Is there a chance we could be friends? I know our parents want us to be more than that, but I wouldn't mind having you as a friend."

"We are friends."

He arched his eyebrow. "I mean *real* friends, Shelby. I would hate to miss an opportunity because our parents insisted on us to make some political statement."

"But I've been so awful. Why would you want to be my friend?"

"Under all that snarkiness, I think you have some soft spots. For example, a completely snarky debutant wouldn't have stuck up for Riley the way you did at our table. Priscilla and Tabitha were awful. I had expected you to be on their side. I think that says a lot about who you are."

"We'll see." It wasn't that I wouldn't be his friend, but it felt too risky. What if he used what he learned about me against me? What if it was just a ploy?

He smiled. "I'll take that ... for now."

I smiled and continued to slow dance. The motion soothed me. My eyes fluttered close as I rested my head on his shoulder. I inhaled his cologne. It didn't offend me as much as before. I listened to the steady thrum of his heart as it calmed my own. It could be nice to trust someone other than myself. The question was, could I let it happen?

～

I peeled off my heels as the last guest had left. My fingers hovered over the skin Luke had kissed on my cheek as he had said goodbye. We had agreed to meet later in the week for coffee. It was a start, nothing like dinner, but it was more than I would have agreed to before tonight. We had danced for what felt like hours, and I had even laughed at his humor by the end. There was hope that something closer to friends could happen.

My mood shattered when I heard the quick clacking of heels against the tile floor. That pace could only belong to one person. I turned in time to see her set her stance, hands on her hips.

"We have some talking to do, Shelby."

I pinched the inside of my palm and straightened, cradling my heels in my arms. "Okay."

Vivian crossed her arms. "Your little display after dinner almost ruined the evening. That girl should not have been here. I will ensure she never attends one of my functions again."

My eyebrow rose in response. "Why? What is so horrendous about Riley Mills that she can't be seen in this house?"

"Her parents are separated."

"And ...? This is the twenty-first century, Mother. Divorce happens."

"Well, not if one can mind it. You don't see many upstanding families separating."

"Okay ... Doesn't mean it doesn't happen."

"She was also born out of wedlock."

"*Ooh.* Scandalous."

Vivian glared. "You would do best to mind your tone with me, young lady."

I straightened. "It's still nothing *she* did, Mother."

"Do I have to remind you that you are who you associate

with? We don't associate with families like that. Even if it isn't directly her fault, it is her family's fault, and it would still affect us."

"Fine." I internally rolled my eyes. It took all my strength not to actually do it. If she saw with the mood she was in, I would be more than screwed.

Her scowl lightened. "But your dancing with Luke seemed to set things straight with our guests, so I can forgive your mishap with that unfortunate girl."

"How generous of you."

Mother pointed at me. "Don't get smart with me, young lady."

I raised my hands in self-defense. "I'm sorry. I didn't mean it."

"That's better." Mother surveyed the foyer. "Hmm, how come your friends didn't stay over tonight? They usually stay for breakfast and then go home."

"I wasn't feeling like company tonight."

"Very well. It will be easier to clean without having guests. I expect you up early for Christmas breakfast."

"Okay—"

A loud bang startled me.

My mother and I both turned toward the sound.

Within seconds, my father descended the stairs, briefcase and luggage in hand.

I knitted my brows. Why was he packed? He had just arrived home barely six hours ago.

"Thaddeus?" my mother asked in almost a whisper.

"Ah, good. You're here. It saves me from sending you an email." My father checked his watch then eyed the two of us. "I must go. I'll be gone for a few days."

"Gone?" I asked.

"Again?" my mother added.

He nodded.

My mother twisted her wedding band around her finger. "But why? It's Christmas Eve. What about tomorrow morning? What about our family traditions?"

My father sighed. "Send me a photo when Shelby opens whatever you got her. Business relations are important. I can't miss this trip."

"But who is *honestly* working when it's Christmas Eve!" my mother shouted. "Everyone is with their families. What are you telling the people you see?" My mother took a few steps closer to him then stopped. Barely audible, "What about me?"

"Vivian, please don't be so dramatic."

"Dramatic?"

My mother's shrill voice ran through me. It wasn't a frustration shrill; it was the shrill that only surfaced when she was hurt. I had only heard it a few times growing up, but I knew that sound anywhere. It echoed my own heartache.

This was supposed to be a time for us to be together. Christmas, by definition, was a holiday of giving and receiving. How could someone give anything if they weren't present? How could he receive our love if he was somewhere else? Why didn't he want to stay? He was president of Rowe Industries. He called the shots. He didn't do anything he didn't want to do, so why would he want to do this?

I watched without comprehending what my parents said. Their voices rose, but all I heard was buzzing. I couldn't take it. Not after everything else. I slowly backed away on my tiptoes until I was in the kitchen, entirely by myself.

I took the backstairs to my room and shut the door. The second the latch clicked in the doorjamb, a sob erupted from my chest. I almost didn't know it was from me. It sounded foreign. I never cried, and yet, here I was sobbing on Christmas Eve.

I crumpled onto the rug in my bedroom unable to move

or breathe. How did everything feel so broken? How could things be this bad? Something was amiss between my parents. My aunt and mother couldn't stop fighting, and I was target practice for them all. Any and all emotional baggage fell square on my shoulders.

Who was here for me? Who was here to lift my baggage? It weighed me down like cinderblocks—crushing me.

A soft knock emanated from my bedroom door, but I didn't have the strength to answer. Arms embraced me then rocked me until the sobbing stopped. Hands stroked my hair while my aunt hummed a lullaby.

I sniffed and wiped away the tears with the back of my hand.

My aunt lifted my chin and stared into my eyes. "What's the matter, Shelby?"

I caught the sight of my face in my closet mirror and cringed. My makeup streaked my face and smeared under my eyes. "Mother and Father were fighting."

"Again?"

"Yep, he left tonight for another few days."

Delilah inhaled deeply. "I'm so sorry. Did he say why?"

"Business, or something." I shook my head. "I couldn't listen for too long. It was too much."

She nodded sympathetically. "Well, it's okay. I'm here. Can I help you?"

"No. I'll figure it out."

"Are you sure?"

"Yeah, it's fine." A sniffle echoed through my body, an aftershock from the sobbing. "Where were you tonight? I barely saw you."

"Here and there. I know how to sneak out."

I cracked a half smile. "You should have taken me with you."

"Can't do. Your mother would have noticed. You were a

guest of honor; I am a simple sister with a forgettable last name. No one would notice my whereabouts."

"I did."

She lovingly tapped her index finger to my nose. "Well, no one besides you." She squeezed me tight. "I love you."

I squeezed back. "I love you too."

She stood and helped me to my feet. "See you in the morning?"

"Yep, bright and early to help clean."

"I'll stay with you. We can get through this together."

"Thanks, Aunt Delilah."

"Always."

She squeezed through the small opening in the doorway and gently closed the door behind her.

I trudged to my bathroom and unraveled the toilet paper. I blew hard and threw away the tissue. Aimlessly, I reached for my makeup removal wipes, pulled one out and rubbed as hard as I could. The motion soothed me somehow. With each wipe, I took off the makeup and rubbed away the pain from that evening.

It hadn't all ended up being bad. I needed to hold onto that. I could get through Christmas break, and when school started again, it would be enough distraction that I didn't have to worry. I would be fine ... I had to be.

I put on the rattiest pajamas I owned—which, if I'm being honest, wasn't that bad—and crawled into bed. The comfort of my down comforter enveloped me in warmth as it lulled me to sleep.

CHAPTER 13

*T*he morning sun shone through my open curtains. I rubbed my eyes and sighed. It felt like I had just gone to bed. I slapped my nightstand, searching for my phone, when my hand landed on the familiar case. I pulled it toward me and unlocked it. The bright screen made me squint as I checked the time—seven o'clock on the dot.

I yawned and kicked the covers off me. I nearly tripped over the large packages strewn in the middle of my floor.

"What the …?" I said to no one in particular.

I blinked several times, hoping to clear the picture in front of me. *All* my presents sat on the floor by my bed. This was new, even for my mother. We usually had breakfast then gathered by the large Christmas tree in the ballroom and opened whatever gifts were there. What was going on? Had I slept through Christmas and not realized it?

I snatched my phone from my bed and checked the date. Nope, it was Christmas.

Great, if this was how my day would begin, how would the rest of it go?

I snuck into the hallway and grabbed a few towels from

the closet then ran to my bathroom. A shower would wake me up, and, if that didn't work, I would get coffee.

Showered and dressed in jeans and my favorite navy-colored cardigan, I descended the stairs. As expected, my mother was in the ballroom dressed to the nines and ordering around the staff.

I cleared my throat. "Mom? Why are packages on the floor of my bedroom? Aren't we having breakfast?"

My mother spun around, eyebrows fixed, lips pursed. "Of course, we're having breakfast. I needed to get this room cleaned up. The packages were in the way."

"But aren't we going to open them together?"

Vivian rolled her eyes. "Aren't you a little old for us to go through that charade? You can open them when you feel like it. Make sure to discard the wrapping paper and keep your room clean. I don't want it to look like a pigsty."

I gulped hard. What was happening? This whole Christmas break felt unreal. My father was missing, my mother wanted to erase every chance of happiness, and my aunt still hid in her room.

"Sure, of course. What can I do?"

She waved me off. "Make yourself busy until breakfast. It will be sharply at nine o'clock."

My stomach rolled in anticipation. That was over an hour away. What would I do until then?

My mother didn't see anything. She didn't see me stalk up the stairs. She didn't see me close my bedroom door. And she certainly didn't see my eyes well up.

I sat surrounded by the heap of presents on the floor. How was it possible I wasn't even in the mood to open them? I hadn't asked for anything, and even if I had, I would give it all back now just to spend quality time with my parents. This wasn't supposed to be how today went. It wasn't supposed to be how any days went, and yet this reality seemed to encroach on more and more of my life.

I stood suddenly, causing the blood to rush and unsteady me. I refused to let their sour attitudes ruin my Christmas. I would just find someone else to spend it with.

An unexpected buzz from my phone stopped me cold. Who would send me a message this early? I checked the message ID. It wasn't anyone in my contacts. My face contorted in confusion. The message read, *Merry Christmas, Shelby! I hope you have a good day.*

Who would send me that? And more importantly, why weren't they in my contacts. I had everyone in my contacts. I replied, *Who's this?*

It's Luke.

Luke was texting me? How did he even get my number?

Your mother gave me your number in case I couldn't find you in the stables. She wanted to make sure we had connected before the ball.

I rolled my eyes. Of course, my mother would give him my number.

Oh, well, thanks. Merry Christmas to you too. I tossed the phone on my bed and watched as it hopped from the force, then I treaded down the hallway toward my aunt's room. At the large bedroom door, I knocked.

It was soft, but within seconds, my aunt called, "Come in!"

I opened the door and stared. She wore a burgundy sweater dress with her hair up in a messy bun. She looked comfy and stylish all at once. How did she do that?

Delilah beamed as I entered. "Merry Christmas!"

I smiled. "Merry Christmas."

Delilah scrunched her nose. "You don't sound very cheerful."

I shrugged. "I'm trying to not let them get to me, but

Mother is in a serious mood. She had the staff send all my gifts to my room this morning."

Delilah's eyes widened. "Oh, man."

"Exactly. I don't know what's going on with them, but this is nuts. We're family; why can't we have a normal holiday together like we used to? I just want quality time. I don't want the stupid presents."

My aunt stroked my cheek. "I'm so sorry, Shelby. I wish I could make it better." Her eyes lit up, and her sparkle returned. "Actually, that's exactly what I'll do. We must go to breakfast I'm sure, but afterward, I'm taking you out. We'll go have fun and enjoy this holiday."

"On Christmas? Nothing in Honey Cove is open, except maybe Morgan's Market."

She smirked. "You just leave that up to me. We'll have a blast."

"If you say so."

Aunt Delilah nudged my shoulder. "So, what did you get?"

I shrugged.

She gasped then giggled. "Are you telling me you didn't open them yet?"

"Why would I? I didn't ask for anything."

Aunt Delilah bounded through the doorway. "So? You coming?"

I laughed and followed her to my bedroom. "I'm sure it's clothes, a purse, maybe a pair of shoes."

"Well, can't hurt to look."

I rolled my eyes. "I think you just want to know."

"Maybe ..."

"Okay, okay fine. We can open them."

She clapped and sat on the floor. "Which one should we start with?"

I sat next to her. "I don't care. Just pick one and open it." I surveyed the large and small boxes scattered across my floor.

I picked a medium-sized box from the middle of the pile with shiny red wrapping paper and a silver ribbon. I shook it gently and listened. It had a quiet thud, but nothing rattled or jangled. My guess was that it contained clothes.

I slowly peeled away the paper then undid the tape that held the box closed. As suspected, it was a sage green cashmere sweater. I felt the soft material as I twisted it between my thumb and forefinger. The material was exquisite, but it still didn't make up for the numbing feeling of being invisible and unimportant.

My aunt's tongue peeked out as she concentrated on unwrapping the package she had chosen. The box was smaller, and jingling noises emanated from within as she wrestled with the difficult paper. I stifled a giggle as she finally removed the ribbon and paper. The box was that perfect shade of turquoise and, like I thought, it contained jewelry.

She pried open the box and revealed a new set of earrings and matching ring, all in deep purple. Again, another beautiful gift, but they were just things; they didn't replace the love I craved.

"Oh, these are gorgeous, Shelby," Delilah said as she prominently displayed the opened box in her hand.

I showed her my find.

She reached over to rub the sweater. "I love the feel of cashmere—so buttery and soft on my skin."

"Yeah, it's nice."

"Cheer up, kiddo. We've got more to open."

She was right; I did have several more to open. I just didn't care what any of them contained. At the end of the day, my parents weren't spending time with me, and that tainted any joy I could feel from unwrapping a present.

∼

pening presents had taken longer than I expected. We managed to finish unwrapping just in time for breakfast. In total, I had received three other sweaters, a winter dress, two pairs of boots, a new purse, the earrings and ring, and a few other odds and ends like notebooks and fancy pens.

"Wow," Delilah said.

"Pretty usual."

She laughed and playfully tapped my arm. "Not for everyone."

I smiled. "Yes, you're right. I'm grateful. I am, I just would have rather had memories or moments with them, not the stuff."

She stroked her chin. "So, what you're saying is I can have this all, and you won't care?"

"Go for it."

Delilah chuckled. "I'm kidding, but good to know. I doubt we are the same size."

I eyed her. "I think you'd fit. We look about the same size."

"Maybe, but I'm not going to take your stuff, Shelby."

I shrugged.

She pulled my hand and helped me stand. "Come here. You have one more."

I arched my eyebrow. "We have to get down to breakfast."

"It won't take long."

I followed her to her room.

She searched through a few bags and retrieved two small boxes.

She handed me one to start. I unwrapped the corner and grinned wide when I saw the deck of cards underneath—more specifically, a pinochle deck.

"Thank you! This is perfect. I need to practice."

"You're welcome. Now open this one."

I set the deck of cards on her dresser and took the other package from her hand. Something slid around as I unwrapped the paper that covered the box. I lifted the top half and revealed a silver horse keychain. It was a paint, just like my Rio. I clutched it to my chest. "This looks like Rio. I love it!" I closed the distance between us and hugged her.

She rubbed my back as we hugged. "I'm glad you like them both. They aren't much, but I wanted to get you a little something."

"It's perfect. I love them more than anything else I had in that room."

Delilah smiled. "Let's get to breakfast. We don't want to cross your mother anymore today."

We walked side by side down the hallway and stopped at my room to put the keychain and deck of cards with the others then took the stairs to the dining room.

When we arrived, my mother sat poised in her chair at the head of the table. She sipped something warm as the steam radiated from the top of her mug. She glanced at us both as we took our seats. "Merry Christmas."

"Merry Christmas, Mother."

"Merry Christmas, Vivian."

"Thank you for the presents."

"You're welcome."

"I'm starving. I can't wait for food," I said, trying to cut the tension.

"Yes, I could eat a good meal myself," Delilah said.

My mother continued to sip her drink.

I wanted to slouch and whine about how ridiculous this whole thing was, but, if I expected to repair any of this holiday with my mother, I needed to sit up straight and use my manners. Anything less and I could forget it.

After sitting in silence for what felt like ten hours, Mr. Bennet placed plates of food on the table. I surveyed the options. There was a large plate with scrambled eggs, a plate with bacon and sausage, strawberry and banana filled crepes, French toast, and waffles.

I inhaled the wonderful scent of the food, and my stomach gurgled in anticipation. My mouth salivated, and I couldn't wait to dig in, but first I had to wait. My mother would take what she wanted before we could choose what we wanted.

Mother scanned the food options as she sipped her drink. She didn't grab a plate and serve herself. She didn't look at either of us. She sipped until I thought it was absolutely impossible she had anything left in her cup. Finally, she grabbed a plate and put one crepe on it and picked up her fork.

I noticed my aunt's face was scrunched up like mine. With all these choices, was she really only going to choose a *single* crepe?

I shrugged, and we both grabbed our plate. I piled a little bit of everything onto my plate and made sure to avoid my mother's gaze. She would disapprove of a lady eating so much, but I didn't care. Why let it go to waste just because she wanted me to have a ridiculous-sized figure?

I took a mouthful of bacon and smiled, satisfied, as the pleasant sounds of crunching overtook my senses. It was salty and savory and all things delicious. Bacon was rare in our house. It was only an option on special occasions, and I ensured to take advantage of it any chance I could get.

"Mother, last night was a beautiful evening. You did a great job."

"Thank you, Shelby. It turned out all right. All things considered."

I gulped. "Priscilla and Tabitha thought so as well. They wondered how you would ever top it."

"I always find a way."

"Yes, you do." I eyed both and nudged Aunt Delilah under the table.

"Yes, very beautiful Vivian."

"I'm glad you enjoyed it, Delilah. A glimpse of what you could be doing if you applied yourself."

I sucked in a deep breath. Could nothing either of them say to each other be nice? Thankfully, Delilah didn't retort.

"I agree, Vivi. Maybe next year I'll help you plan."

My mother froze with her mug midway in the air. "That would be nice." She replaced the mug on the table and continued to eat.

I mouthed, *Thank you*, to my aunt and finished my breakfast. The faster we finished, the faster I could have our day of fun.

~

"You saved my life, Aunt Delilah."

"Oh, it was no big deal."

I shook my head. "Yes, it is. That breakfast was unbearable."

Delilah sighed. "It's honestly a shame that your mother is acting like that. She's so much worse than I remembered."

"I still can't imagine a warmer version of her."

"That's tragic."

"Maybe, but it's true."

I buttoned my coat and wrapped the scarf around my neck. I had changed my slippers for thick socks and my knee-high fur boots. It wasn't freezing out yet, but I had no idea where my aunt planned to go, and I certainly didn't want to become cold.

"Can we make a stop at the stables? I want to give Rio some carrots and apples for Christmas."

"Of course."

I opened the large front doors.

Aunt Delilah closed them behind me, and we trekked to the stables side by side.

"What else was she like when you both were younger?"

Delilah smiled and twisted her scarf around her finger. "Wild."

My eyes bulged. "Wild? No way."

Delilah giggled. "Yep, she was a free spirit. Wild and fun-loving."

"Really? I can't picture that at all. What happened?"

"I suppose we all have to grow up. Like I told you before, she was never the same after that day."

"No … that's more than just growing up. That's an entirely different person. I have never seen her be wild a day in my life. Haunted or not, she can't be happy with her life. She's horrid."

"I don't really know. As we got older, we stopped being close. I traveled, and she went to college then married your father. Things changed, and we continued to drift."

"That's so sad. I wish it wasn't just me. It must have been nice having someone else by your side."

"It was nice when it was good. But having that person turn on you doesn't feel so great either." Aunt Delilah shrugged. "I suppose that same Vivi is deep down somewhere."

Could Aunt Delilah be right? I couldn't imagine my mother being fun-loving and wild. She was poised and rigid, the absolute opposite of what Aunt Delilah described. There had to be more to the story than what Aunt Delilah told me. Could one day really change someone so much?

We arrived at the stables, and my aunt waited outside.

I found Rio at the back of the stables in his stall, eating hay and oats. I rubbed his nose. "Hey, boy. Merry Christmas. Do you want some treats?"

He whinnied.

"I'll take that as a yes."

I dumped the bag of sliced apples and carrots into his bucket and watched as he devoured them one by one.

"Be good, boy. I'll be back to ride you soon."

He whinnied and shook his head.

I buttoned my coat and walked back toward Aunt Delilah.

She was waiting patiently at the doors and smiled when she caught sight of me. "Ready?"

"All set."

We walked to her rental, and she fiddled with the radio until she found a station that wasn't playing Christmas music. It sounded like an eighties station, but I didn't mind. It would be nice to get out of the house and feel a little lighter.

"So, did you leave anyone behind to come visit us?"

My aunt chuckled. "Is that your subtle way of asking if I'm dating someone?"

"Maybe."

"Well, no. I am not seeing anyone back home."

"By choice or …?"

She shrugged as she focused on the road. "It's not necessarily on purpose."

"I understand that."

"Do you? You and that Luke boy seemed cozy at the ball last night."

"We were acting."

Delilah arched an eyebrow in response. "Acting? That looked like a lot more than acting. I think you're warming up to him."

"Me? No. He might not be quite as vapid as I thought, but nothing is happening between us. He did text me this morning though. It was certainly unexpected."

"Do you want more to happen?"

"No. I can't deal with that right now. My parents are enough drama to keep me busy."

She smirked. "While that is difficult, you don't need to take responsibility for it. You can still be a teenager *and* enjoy the company of a particular boy."

"Thanks, Aunt Delilah, but I'll pass."

"Fair enough."

"Do you ever miss living in Honey Cove?"

"Not at all."

"How come?"

"I wasn't built for small towns. I need more in life—more diversity, more space. Honey Cove is cramped and can be small-minded. I didn't want that kind of life as an adult."

"Will you at least visit more?"

"Yes, and I'm not leaving right away, but yes. I'll make sure to not wait so long before I visit you again."

I stared out the window as the farms passed by, and town became closer. How free Aunt Delilah must have felt to leave and go somewhere else. I couldn't say I wanted to leave Honey Cove per se, but I knew I felt stifled by my parents. If something didn't change, I didn't know how I could continue on this path without some sort of change.

I cleared my throat. "Where are we going?"

She smiled. "You'll see."

I sighed and leaned back in my seat, listening to the eighties music and being thankful I wasn't at home in my room or playing mediator for my mother and literally anyone else.

We parallel parked on a side street by the park. I squinted as I looked outside the car window. I had no idea what we could be doing in this part of town. Of course, the park was open, but did she expect to walk around?

I exited her rental and brushed off my jeans as I waited for her to lock the car. I stared at the streetlamps that lined the street, displaying wreaths and red ribbons with garland wrapped around the pole. Only snow was missing to perfect the image. Except, we wouldn't get snow now, maybe not even at all, but certainly not this early.

"This way," my aunt said.

I followed behind her. The sky was clear and a pale blue as the sun shone on us. The park was devoid of many people. Only an older couple sat on one of the benches at the far end of the park.

Delilah stopped suddenly, and I tried to avoid bumping her. In front of us was a dark-colored carriage draped with holiday décor and with two white horses.

"A carriage ride?" I asked.

"Yes! It'll be so much fun, don't you think?"

I nodded. It would certainly be an adventure. I hopped into the carriage, noticing the pine fragrance, and hoped the nagging feeling of everything else would go away.

CHAPTER 14

I hustled toward the diner as thoughts of the last few days circled my mind. The carriage ride and subsequent stroll with my aunt had helped a little but not as much as I had hoped. When we had returned to the house, my mother was nowhere to be found. I spent the rest of that evening and the following day hiding in my bedroom as much as possible.

Surprisingly, my mother didn't make a fuss out of it, which terrified me even more. She had never let me have that much freedom or time locked away in my room. Even when I had work to do for school, I had to show my face and appear in certain situations. I couldn't dwell too long on what would cause her to lax on such a thing.

The door rang as I entered Over Easy's, our local diner. I didn't frequent any place in town too often, but it was the best place for coffee. Honey Cove was full of mom-and-pop businesses, not fancy restaurants or beverage chains.

I surveyed the customers for my coffee date. On the left side of the diner near the front sat Luke Warrington. I smiled as our gazes met. I had to admit something had shifted since the Christmas ball, and it was nice not to have to hate him, even if it was only a little less.

I plopped on the seat and unraveled my pashmina scarf. "Hey, Luke."

He smiled wide, revealing the dimple on his left cheek. "Hey yourself."

Had he always had dimples? Or had I been so keen on ignoring any of his features that I hadn't noticed before?

"Thank you for this. I needed to get out."

Luke arched his eyebrow. "Everything okay?"

"Eh. Things just feel so off lately. Have you ordered yet?"

"Nope. I was waiting for you."

I pulled off my coat and set it over the chair. "Awesome. I need something to warm me up."

Luke chuckled. "It isn't even freezing yet."

"So? I can be cold in sixty-degree weather."

"Is that so? Must be a chick thing."

I stuck out my tongue. "Or it's just getting colder, and I'm not used to it."

"Fair enough. Maybe you need a thicker coat."

"Hush. I'll survive once I get some hot chocolate or a latte."

"True, although I'm starving. I might need to actually order food."

"Go for it. I don't come here much though, so not sure what they have foodwise."

Luke's eyes widened. "No? A Rowe who doesn't venture into the town's local cuisine? How scandalous."

"I know, I know. It's not because I haven't wanted to, I just don't get the chance. We have our own chef. How am I supposed to say I need to go out when he would cook me anything?"

"That's a tragedy. Over Easy's has good food."

"I'll keep that in mind."

An older man stopped at our table. "Welcome to Over Easy's. Name's Roger. What can I get you?"

"I'll take a coffee, black, and your cowboy burger, well-done, extra barbeque sauce," Luke said.

Roger scribbled on his notebook then looked to me.

"I'll start with some hot chocolate, if that's okay."

"Sure thing. I'll be right back with your drinks."

"So how was your Christmas? I was surprised by your text."

"Great. I spent it with my family all day. We opened presents, had breakfast, then we have a tradition; we pick one boardgame each and have to play them all."

I smiled. "That sounds really nice."

Luke shrugged. "It's nice. I'm sure you did something less dorky. Not everyone is into boardgames."

"Boardgames aren't dorky. They can be hilarious if you play with the right people." I shuffled the sugar packets and fidgeted with my scarf. "I wouldn't say I did anything better than your day."

"Being modest, are we? Let's hear it. What'd you do?"

"Honestly? My presents had been delivered to my room before I woke up. I opened them with my aunt before we went for a breakfast as silent as the woods in the winter. My aunt took me to the park for a carriage ride and a little stroll, but that was it."

I peeked at Luke's face, trying to read his expression. I didn't really know him well. I didn't even know if it was safe and okay to talk to him about these things. He could take what he found out and use it against me. Heck, he could still be using me, and I wouldn't know.

Luke reached for my hand and squeezed. "I'm sorry, Shelby. I had no idea. Your life always seems so glamorous."

I snorted as Roger set our mugs on the table. "That's the

way it's supposed to look. But I get shuffled from one event to another without anyone asking if it's what I wanted."

"I understand that. Spending most of my year at a boarding school kind of sucks. I have friends there, but it's all about grooming us to be high-functioning members of our societies. It's not about who we are as people, yanno?"

"Definitely. My life is completely like that, minus the boarding school. Which sometimes I think could be nice. You get to leave this town and all the expectations people throw onto you."

"Yeah, but you also have to go to places where no one cares about you and are only out for themselves. At least here, you have some familiarity and comfort."

"I suppose. Depends on if you have anyone here who does that for you."

Luke arched an eyebrow. "No true friends?"

I shook my head. "Everyone expects me to be this southern debutante with her life together and being charitable to the right people and downright awful to others who aren't deemed worthy. I mean, how messed up is that?"

"Wow."

"What?"

Luke chuckled. "I had no idea we were this similar. I'll admit I thought that's exactly who you were until…"

"Until what?"

Luke averted his gaze and stared into his coffee. Had he felt the shift too? "The ball when we actually talked, the real you and me."

"I thought it was just me who felt the shift."

"No, I did too. I wouldn't have invited someone like that to get coffee."

"No? You hounded me pretty hard to pull off our ball operation."

"I had to. My parents expect certain things from me too, and to have an offer come from the Rowes, you don't take no for an answer. They couldn't go, but what better way for that to be overlooked than for the son to attend the ball. My hands were tied just as much as yours."

I rolled my eyes. "See, that's just it. Why does my family have all this power? So what, my father's company has hundreds of employees and gives money to charities and supports the community? What makes him or us so damn special to act like we are royalty?"

Luke shrugged. "That's just the way it's always been."

"Well, I don't like it. If someone has that much power, they should be using it to help others. To be genuinely altruistic. This half-and-half nonsense is sickening, and I'm tired of it."

Luke grinned, flashing his perfect dimple. "Then change it."

I peered into my hot chocolate and contemplated his proposal. He hadn't been the first to say that. Riley, Randy, and several people at this point had told me the same thing. What if I did change how others saw the Rowes? What if I changed how things were done? How would people take it, and would they even listen to me?

"Hey, don't do that," Luke said.

I peered up to gaze into his perfectly hazel eyes. "Do what?"

"Doubt your power."

I smiled. "Who says I have any power?"

"You and I both know you do. You've shown me glimpses of it this whole time. You just need to decide what you want to do and who you want to be. Otherwise, why kill yourself about your image?"

"True."

I had to admit he had a point, and I enjoyed our banter. Never in a million years did I think I could have a genuine conversation with Luke Warrington. Maybe his image was just as flawed as mine was.

Roger dropped Luke's burger and fries on the table. "Would you like anything else, ma'am?"

"I'll take another hot chocolate if you don't mind."

"Sure thing."

Luke stared at his food, mouthwatering like a dog in a treat store.

"You excited?"

Luke met my gaze. "Was I drooling?"

I laughed. "Just a little."

"It's just so good. You must try it."

I shook my head. "I'm okay. Thanks though."

"You sure?" he asked as he wiggled his eyebrows.

"Positive."

He took a huge bite of his burger, and when he pulled away, his chin was slathered in barbeque sauce.

I couldn't contain the giggles. "You have a little something …"

Luke smirked and dabbed his face with his napkin. "Better?"

I nodded. I could never eat a burger like that. The mess alone would deter me—but his fries, now those looked delicious.

While Luke was midbite, I snatched a fry from his plate and plopped it in my mouth.

He gasped, and his eyes bulged. "Did you just take a fry?"

I quickly chewed and muttered, "Maybe."

He chuckled. "You did!"

I swallowed the last bit. "It was good though."

"That's okay. I'll share some, but don't eat 'em all. I would be too sad to not have my burger and fries."

I raised my hand and crossed my heart. "I promise."

Our gazes locked, and I could have sworn my stomach felt fluttery. Maybe I was hungrier than I thought? Because there was no way the flutters had anything to do with Luke.

How was it possible that Luke Warrington could grow on me this much in a few days? By the time our coffee-food get together was nearing an end, I couldn't help smiling at his humor.

"I've had a nice time," Luke said.

"Me too. When do you have to go back to school?"

"I have five days left."

Five days? That seemed impossibly short. I had hoped we could see if friends would be possible, but five days seemed like too short of a time.

"Are you going to the next Founder's meeting?"

"No. My dad doesn't have me go to those yet. He's more focused on my schooling. He says when I get to college, we'll talk. I'm fine with that. Why be in those stuffy board meetings to begin with?"

I laughed. "True, although I don't have the choice. Randy and I must give our proposal to the board to improve tourism. I'm worried about how it will go. Those men don't listen to me, and Randy doesn't have clout."

Luke stared into my eyes. "Then make them listen. You're a Rowe after all; use your power. They certainly would use it against you if the roles were reversed."

Luke had a point. He seemed to understand my world better than most. Tabitha and Priscilla should have been easy confidants, considering it was their world as well, but, for whatever reason, they didn't have the same pressures. Or they did and they handled them differently. I guess I couldn't blame them entirely; I used to be like them too. I hadn't worried about what I was doing to others and how it made them feel. I had figured it was my birthright to say what I thought and do what I felt. If others got hurt, that was their problem, not mine.

If it hadn't been for Riley moving to town and showing me that I could be someone else without all the expectations, I don't know what I would have thought.

We stood from the table and walked through the front doors. I watched as people whispered, no doubt recognizing that founding families were out and about and that we seemed cozy at our table. The gossip trains would be running rampant soon with so called *juicy details* of our encounter.

My keys jingled in my hands. "I'll text you, now that I know it's you."

Luke smiled, his dimple prominent. "I'd like that. I'm glad we are trying to be friends, Shelby. I'm glad you aren't just some southern belle like everyone thinks. You might be surprised; more people are attracted to honey than vinegar."

I smirked. "Bee humor, huh?"

"I've got to! How can't you like a little bee humor? But seriously, I think you'd be surprised by how many people would like this Shelby. Think about it."

"I will. Talk to you soon." I opened my door and sat in the front seat.

Luke closed the door, waved and walked away.

Coffee had been nice, something I didn't realize I needed.

My drive home went quick with the circling thoughts. The house remained silent as I snuck up the stairs. I didn't want the good feeling I had from seeing Luke to disappear if I ran into my mother. That was sure to deflate any hope I could have about salvaging the break.

Once I was safely in my room, I kicked off my shoes,

crawled into my bed and snuggled in the covers. I pulled my phone from my back pocket and opened our school's Buzz app. I didn't usually scroll the posts, because it was usually nonsense, but I was curious what everyone was doing. Were they skiing? On vacations at the beach? Staying home? I stared at the screen as I read the posts.

Merry Christmas, y'all.

Say goodbye to homework and hello to videogames.

Tons of photos from people's break flooded the feed. It looked like everyone was having fun even if I hadn't been. In the middle of my scrolling, I noticed the date—December 27. Crap! How did the time go so quickly? Tomorrow was Saturday and the meeting for the proposal.

I closed the Buzz app and scrolled through my contacts for Randy's number. We needed to meet again to discuss our proposal and make final changes. Everything counted on this proposal, and I refused to drop the ball.

I opened a new message. *Randy, are you available to come over? Tomorrow's the big day, and I want to run through what we plan to say.* I bounced my leg as I waited for his response, thankfully I didn't have to wait long.

I can meet you in an hour?

That's perfect. See you then.

True to his word, Randy showed up exactly one hour later. He carried the same green book bag as before. I watched from the window to see when he would arrive, and before he could knock, I met him outside.

"Thanks for coming. I know it was super last minute. I hope I didn't steal you away from a special someone," I said.

Randy eyed me carefully. "I was at home and had just finished a shift at Morgan's. Wasn't a big deal."

"Mm-hmm."

Randy raised an eyebrow. "Are you prying into my personal life, Shelby?"

I giggled. "Not at all. I was just wondering if you had been with Riley."

"I knew who you meant."

"So, she is special to you."

"Of course, she is, but we aren't dating. We are seeing how it is to be friends."

I walked ahead of Randy toward the guesthouse. "Friends? You both are so smitten with each other, why don't you do something about that already?"

"Who says I haven't?"

"Ooh. So, you *did* ask her out."

"No. My life is too chaotic for me to bring anyone else into it. You of all people know that."

"So? There isn't a declaration that says you can't be happy when your parents cause total chaos in your life."

"No, but it wouldn't be fair for anyone else to deal with it just because I wanted to be selfish."

"I suppose you're right. But, if you both like each other, why don't you just go for it?"

Randy rolled his eyes. "Some things are worth taking your time before you get to the destination."

"And this is one of those things?"

He nodded. "I don't want my family stuff to screw up a chance I could or couldn't have with her."

"She's important."

"Absolutely. You know what the town says and does."

"Oh, only too well." I paused. "You and I are the same when it comes to Riley."

Randy scrunched his nose. "How so?"

"She provides us both with a clean slate."

"I guess that's true … or was at first. But Riley is more than that. She makes me want to be better. Do better, every day."

"I understand that."

Randy squinted through the sun as he stared. "She told me about the talk you two had at the ball."

I fiddled with my coat's zipper. Had she mentioned it because she couldn't believe I had apologized again? Or did she finally hear me this time? I kept my gaze forward, waiting for his response. "Oh?"

"Yeah, told me you seemed more sincere this time. And sad." He cleared his throat. "Is everything okay with you?"

"Of course, why?"

Randy stopped walking. "Shelby, you may fool other people, but the loneliness in your eyes calls out to people who are looking."

I shrugged. "Things could be better, I suppose. You know how the expectations and obligations impose on our lives. It feels ten times worse with my parents. They can never decide who I'm supposed to be."

"Did you think about what I said before?"

"Kind of. But how is it easy to just abandon what I've always been taught and know?"

"You aren't. You're abandoning what you *aren't*."

We arrived at the guesthouse door. How was it so easy for Randy to say those things, even with all the drama surrounding his father? I knew better than anyone the stories that circled through town about his father.

He's a drunk.

What a waste.

He's done for it.

Every time I heard a new one, I cringed. It could easily have been my family who had suffered from the bee populations decreasing. The mites weren't biased. They attacked our populations too. The only difference? We had more capital and more bees.

"We should finalize our proposal," I said as I walked through the doorway and sat on the sofa.

Randy eyed me warily.

I knew he wasn't buying my transition, but I couldn't go that deep right now. If I climbed into that hole, I wasn't sure I would come back up. Or worse, I didn't know who I would be when I did climb out.

CHAPTER 15

I waved goodbye as Randy climbed into his truck. We had finished our proposal. We had practiced and had even made a few notecards. Tomorrow would be the only opportunity to show the council we could do this. And not only do it but crush their expectations.

I shivered. When my father found out that Randy not only had most of the ideas but helped throughout the entire process, he would lose his mind. He expected me to do it on my own, and especially not with Randy. But we both needed this, and I wouldn't reject Randy's ideas just because my father deemed it necessary.

Randy's truck disappeared, and I walked back inside. The house was quiet, suspicious. My mother had been missing for too long, and I half expected her to pop out of a closet or a hidden room and scare me just to unleash her emotions. Things were off, and I had no idea what had caused it.

I had trudged halfway up the stairs when the sound of a car door shut. Who would that be? Could my father finally be home?

I turned and stared down at the door as a member of our

staff waited at the door to open it. I peered over the railing to get a better look.

My father strolled through the front door, passed his overcoat to the staff member and dropped his briefcase on the floor for them to pick up.

I stayed still on the stairs, watching his expressions. I had no idea what kind of mood he would be in. He hadn't been home except for several days in over a month. Would he be relaxed and happy to be home? Or would he be restless and fidgety for having to stay?

I stared at his chiseled jaw and combed chestnut hair. I couldn't see it from my spot on the stairs, but I knew his hazel eyes were changing with the lighting and growing darker after being outside. His blank expression gave me no inclination of what kind of mood he was in, and I wanted it to stay that way. One grouchy parent was enough, having two was more than I wanted. Besides, when he found out what I would present, I surely would have two parents angry at me. I didn't want to rush it.

I sat on the stairs, ready to head to my room, when the *click-clack* of heels echoed in the foyer. My father's skin around his eyes tightened, and his neutral expression faded into pursed lips and crossed arms.

"Vivian," my father said.

"Thaddeus, I'm glad to see you got home safely."

"Of course, I did, Vivian. I didn't hire imbeciles."

Vivian's sigh was audible, even from where I sat. Why were they arguing so much lately?

"I didn't mean it like that, Thad. I'm just glad you're safe and home."

"Yes, well I can't miss the founding-family council meeting. Shelby has her proposal, and I wouldn't miss that."

Mother's gaze sharpened, and her lips thinned into a

straight line. "I see. Well, she will be happy to know you're home."

This was so strange. What had happened between them?

"Yes, well, I'll be in my study. I have work to finish before bed."

"You won't have dinner with us?"

"I ate before I got home."

My mother diverted her gaze and stared at the tile. "Okay. Have a good night, dear." She leaned in to kiss his cheek, but he kept walking, ignoring her move.

I stood and tiptoed toward my room. Something was off, and I didn't know what. But there was no way I would ask. Once I was off the stairs and on the landing, I sprinted to my room and shut the door. I would stay in my room all night if it meant I didn't have to deal with whatever was happening with them, not to mention I had an early morning. I needed to sleep and practice my part of the proposal. It had to be perfect.

~

The notecards taunted me as I repeatedly reshuffled them, waiting for the meeting to start. The car ride with my father was short. He asked if I was ready and stayed glued to his phone for the remainder.

My saliva caught in my throat every time I swallowed. This proposal had to go well or … or nothing. It would go well—period, end of story. There was no option for anything else.

I stared at Randy across the table who adjusted his tie every five seconds. He looked the same way I felt—nervous and frightened.

My father sat next to me and drummed his fingers

against the table. If he was nervous about the proposal, he didn't show it outwardly.

I gulped not knowing if that was a good thing or a bad thing. He was used to making proposals and being the center of a board room full of stuffy, old men hanging on his every word.

I wasn't.

When the clock struck nine, Thaddeus stood and cleared his throat. "Welcome, welcome. I hope everyone had a very merry Christmas. I wanted to take a moment to say how happy I am to have seen you all at my wife's wonderful Christmas ball. It was simply magnificent." He shuffled the papers in front of him. "Today's agenda is a little longer, but I know we will push through it." He studied the paper then eyed everyone around the table. "We will begin with the proposal led by my daughter Shelby about increasing tourism from other towns."

I scooted the chair from the table and cleared my throat. "Thank you, Father. I wanted to start this presentation by stating how grateful I am that you all have entrusted me with this important proposal." I eyed Randy across the table. As soon as I invited him to join, my dad would flip out. I knew that, but it was what I had to do. "I didn't do it alone, and I want to invite Randy Walker to join me on this presentation. We worked on it together, and it's just as much as his proposal as it is mine."

I watched as Randy scooted out his chair and stood. My eyes flitted to my father whose knuckles were white. His face had a blank expression, except for the minor crinkle by his right eye. No one else would have noticed, but I was his daughter after all, and it meant he was as mad as I thought he would be.

"Thank you, Shelby. I'm grateful and honored as well to have been given this opportunity."

"We asked ourselves, what is Honey Cove missing? What do families, children, teenagers want that our town doesn't have?"

Randy looked at his card then smiled at the board members. "We can't compete with other towns that are much larger and have more amenities. We don't have the largest beaches or the latest theater."

"But we do have our down-home family appeal. We are a connected community. Those of us who have lived here all our lives know Honey Cove is a unique place to live. People like the connected aspect of our town."

"So, what if outsiders got to feel that connection too?"

"We have proposed several new festivals throughout the year. We invite other towns in the area to join. Once they gain traction, outside folks will see how great this community is." I kept close attention on my father's features. He maintained his poker face, and his knuckles returned to their normal color a little more than before, but was it enough?

"In addition to the festivals, we'll make relationships with large companies in town and outside of town in a general vicinity to make connections through reciprocal transactions. Have corporate team building in Honey Cove. Promote our cove to their families. With the feeling of reciprocity, people will come."

"During the festivals and the team building, we provide them with Honey Cove products from all the companies. It gains the products' exposure and new customers. We propose the first festival should be a spring festival of sorts. We contemplated a winter one, but in order to arrange all of the companies and to plan it successfully, there needs to be more time to gather all the required information and research," I added.

"The tourism and the increase in revenue can be spent in

our community, strengthening it and uniting us further," Randy finished.

We placed our cards on the table and waited.

My father stroked his chin and glanced at the table.

I followed his gaze staring at each man in their suits, wondering what they thought.

Most of the men seemed to have a passive bored expression plastered among their faces. A few smiled, and the rest stared; Randy's father beamed at his son. He appeared to be sober today.

My father's fingers continued to drum against the table.

Randy cleared his throat. "Does anyone have questions?"

Priscilla's uncle spoke first. "Are you suggesting we *give* free samples to these festivals? That's a large loss of profit you're asking for."

Randy shook his head. "We're suggesting you could set up markets with the products, place them in the hotel rooms where the companies stay, place them in front of the large exhibits at the festival. You could even rent tables to others, but the companies get front and center exposure for people to buy at the festival."

"Exactly. No one is giving it away. We're putting it in front of the visitors. We can also base the festivals around our strengths. Sure, close towns know why our town is called Honey Cove, but let's make our small town more well-known again," I added.

"I see," Mr. Tate said.

Mr. Warrington, Luke's father, spoke next. "How do you propose we get started on these festivals? None of us can spare more time to arrange such a feat. You can't just decide to have a spring festival. We need to market and research what would work best with the demographic we wish to entice."

"We understand that, Mr. Warrington." I smiled directly

at him. "Randy and I discussed that first steps would be collecting data from all the companies for their top sellers. You all know your companies the best. Once all the data is in, we plan what activities would best display those features."

"We should also survey the town. Find out what they wish they could do with their families on a beautiful spring day. Then we get the word out, talk to other companies in the area and the surrounding towns. Find ways they could benefit from our festival and invite them," Randy added.

"It will take time to build it up, but within a few festivals, we should be able to see if it's working."

The men stroked their chins and stared at each other around the table. I couldn't be sure, but it might be working. My father would be the sway vote. If he put his stamp of approval on the ideas, everyone else would follow suit. If he didn't, it would crash and burn. But I couldn't read his expression to save my life.

My father stood. "Let's take a vote for moving forward with this proposal."

Mr. Tate stood. "Thaddeus, you haven't told us what you think yet."

I took a deep breath while I focused on maintaining my composure. I didn't want them to know my insides were squirming.

"Well, I, of course, think the idea is fabulous. It was created by a Rowe."

Silas Walker coughed.

I pinched the inside of my palm. This was not the time for Mr. Walker to make it aware to the others that Randy was involved too. If they focused too much attention on it, my father would back out.

"Aye, let's vote," Mr. Tate said.

A few of the men—my father, Silas, and Mr. Tate—raised their arms first. Slowly but surely, every hand went up.

"Then it's settled. We'll continue with the proposal. All data on top sellers should be brought to the next meeting to continue planning."

Randy and I nodded then sat. Our part of the meeting was over. I glanced at Randy and caught his gaze. I smiled and mouthed, *We did it!*

He smiled back.

At least, in the public version of this meeting, the proposal went well. What would happen behind closed doors? Well, I knew that would be a totally different story.

~

My father and I waited side by side for the driver to arrive. He didn't look at me. He didn't speak to me. He stared straight ahead as if we were strangers. This would not be good.

The driver pulled up by the curb and we both got in.

I snuck a sideways glance at my father's face. His gaze glared, and the slight crinkle was a full-on valley now.

I twisted the end of my scarf around my finger over and over as I waited for his response.

"Shelby," my father said in a hiss.

I gulped and resolved to keep my voice steady. "Yes, Father?"

"What were you *thinking* letting Silas's son help you on the proposal? I gave you strict orders to squash his ideas and do it alone."

I gripped the scarf tighter. "I know, but his ideas were good. What was I supposed to do? Listen and then cut him from the presentation."

His head snapped to the side and glared. "Yes, you were. You were told to ditch him at all costs. That family is a speck of dirt on our council. They should have been kicked out when Silas became a lazy drunkard. He doesn't deserve to be on there anymore. And you know by association so are his children. Letting Randy help you. What were you thinking?"

"I thought it was the right thing to do. We may be *superior,* but it doesn't mean we're ruthless."

"Ruthless? What does that have to do with anything, Shelby?" He ran his hands through his hair and gripped his briefcase tighter. "Things happen in those meetings you don't see. And there are members who feel a change should happen. Do you want to be on the wrong side of that change if you keep this up?"

I shook my head.

"Exactly. Getting help from the Walkers was stupid. I expected better of you, Shelby. I gave you a direct order, and you disobeyed it. What's worse, is you did it in front of the most powerful men in the town. They could destroy us if they wanted to."

"Destroy us? Doesn't that seem a bit much?"

"No. We have a duty to uphold by having the Rowe name. If we slack on our responsibilities, then others will take over. This world isn't sunshine and rainbows. Sometimes you must do the dirty things to stay ahead."

I clamped my mouth shut. This wasn't what I wanted to be about. I didn't want to betray someone just to keep up appearances and my hierarchy. It was absolutely absurd. I did the right thing for Randy and for me. His ideas were good— better than I had. Without him, we had no proposal, and I would stand by that decision no matter who called it stupid.

CHAPTER 16

When I didn't respond, my father stopped talking. I could tell he was still pissed at me, but I wouldn't take back something I knew I had done right. Where was the loyalty and the justice in the actions of the people I loved?

Once we arrived, I stomped to the front door. My father trudged behind me, going much slower, after he had collected his belongings and thanked the driver.

My mother awaited us when I opened the front door. Her face scrunched when she caught my expression, followed by my father's. "What happened?"

"Ask your daughter." He handed his coat and briefcase to Mr. Bennet.

My mother crossed her arms. "Well?"

"I did the right thing, and Father doesn't understand it."

Mother looked between us as I crossed my arms. I was done with both of their attitudes.

"I don't understand."

Father glared at me. "She let that Walker boy *help* her on the presentation. He not only helped her write it but he also presented it in front of the board. She was supposed to ditch him and do it herself."

Mother's eyebrows knitted together. "Did the board like the idea?"

He flung his hands into the air and paced the floor. "That's not the point, Vivian! The Walkers are a tainted family, and by association, she will taint our name and family!" He sighed. "Yes, they liked the proposal. We agreed to move forward with the planning. But I will have to do damage control with some of the other board members."

Mother narrowed her eyes at me. "You let that Walker boy present, knowing it was against your father's wishes?"

"Yes. I did. He had decent—"

"I don't care what he had, Shelby. Your father asked you to do something, and you should have done it. What is with you lately? You keep going against us both." She spread her arms in front of her. "Do we not do enough for you? Do we not give you everything you want? Set you up with the finest families and make sure you are a polished young lady?"

"It's not about that."

Father stared blankly at us both, as if he was too upset to focus on one specific emotion.

Mother crossed her arms. "It is about that, Shelby. You act like a spoiled little brat when you go off on your own. We tell you to do things to protect your future. You would rather associate with the Walker boy and that Riley Mills. You're going to drive this family into the ground."

I huffed. "No. I may actually resurrect some decent Rowe family members. Neither of them did anything to deserve such harsh treatment. Riley has no stake in what her parents did and neither does Randy."

Father shook his head. "Yes, they do. Those kids are the products of their parents. Which means when they do things, people judge the *whole* family. So, when you screw up, we suffer as well."

"So, you'd rather be known as a bunch of cutthroat people than a family that makes decisions based on what's best for the community and the benefit of all?"

"We do what's best for this family, Shelby. Nothing more, nothing less," my father said.

Mother stepped toward me. "I don't know what has gotten into you, but you better fix it fast. I knew when Tabitha and Priscilla came to me about that *Riley Mills* and your fixation on her something had to change."

My brain screeched to a halt. "What?"

"That's right. Your best friends were worried about you changing and came to me. Well, when I heard about that girl, I knew I recognized the last name. I remember her father and her filthy mother. She wasn't good for him. She was beneath him. After a little searching online, I saw everything else. I gave them the information, and I'm glad I did. They actually did what they knew was best for this family." She narrowed her gaze. "Unlike you."

My skin felt hot, and my gaze was blurry. How could she do that? How could they have done that to me?

My mother pointed at me. "I'm telling you what, Shelby. If you don't get your act together, you won't like what I do about it." She turned on her heels and stalked from the foyer.

My father shook his head and followed.

I had known it would be bad. I had known my father would be upset, but I had never expected to hear what I had just heard from them both. I had no idea who those people were, but they certainly weren't the parents I thought they had been.

～

I stomped up the stairs and wiped my eyes. This whole break got worse and worse every day. I passed the door to my bedroom and meandered down the rest of the hallway, scuffing my boots on the floor as I went. I found myself standing in front of my aunt's door, knocking.

She peered through the doorway from the small crack she had opened. "Shelby?" She opened the doorway more and gave me a good once over. "What's wrong?"

I sniffled. "I don't want to talk about the details. I wondered if I could borrow your rental?"

"Sure." She grabbed the key with an orange ring from her nightstand. "Are you sure I can't help?"

"I'm sure. I need to get out of the house without being in my car. It's too noticeable, and I don't want the attention right now."

She squeezed my shoulder.

I turned once the keys hit my palm and walked away. I could feel her eyes on me until I reached the corner for the stairs. I slunk down them, not wanting to alert anyone to my departure. I'd had enough scolding for the day. I walked behind the house and hopped in the rental. I wasn't sure where I was going, but anywhere would be better than here.

At the end of the driveway, I chose left toward town and turned up the radio. Most of the stations were still leftover Christmas songs. I tuned it until I found a pop station that played non-holiday tunes.

As I drove through town, I watched as other couples and families walked arm in arm toward the park into Morgan's Market. They smiled and laughed. I wished that could have been my family, then suddenly I knew where I would go.

Once I was outside the town limits, I headed to the farm lined with cherry trees. The lane was long and decorated here and there with wreaths and mums for the holiday season. When I pulled up to the massive farmhouse over-looking the fields, my stomach dropped. What if they weren't happy to see me here? What if they told me to leave?

I took a deep breath of fresh air and approached the farmhouse. I knocked lightly and surveyed the porch, watching as the swing swayed in the breeze.

A familiar face opened the door and stared at me through the screen. "Shelby? What are you doing here?"

I smiled at Riley. "I hope I'm not imposing too much, but I was hoping I could come in and see your mom-mom?"

Riley's eyes bulged. "My mom-mom?" Then she narrowed her gaze. "Why?"

From behind Riley, a shuffling noise emanated down the hallway, followed by a shout, "Who is it, Riles?"

I sucked in a deep breath as Riley's mom came forward.

Mrs. Mills stared at me through skeptical eyes. "Who is this, Riley?"

I coughed. "I'm Shelby Rowe, Mrs. Mills. I was wondering if I could talk to Mrs. Brooks?"

Riley and her mother exchanged glances, but I couldn't decide how they would proceed. They seemed to be surprised at my arrival, which I couldn't blame them for, but I really wanted to talk to Penny. I had a feeling she would understand my situation better than most.

Mrs. Mills looked down the hallway. "Momma, you have a visitor."

Penny came to the door, wiping her hands on a dish towel. "Shelby. Hello, dear."

Riley's jaw slackened, and Mrs. Mills's eyes widened.

"How do you two know each other, Mom-mom?" Riley asked.

"We … uh. My aunt took me to play cards, and she ended up being there," I answered.

"You play cards?" Riley asked.

"A little."

Penny grasped her coat from the hanger and followed me onto the porch.

Mrs. Mills and Riley stared at me through the screen door.

Penny glared at them, and they quickly shut the door, staring through the small window at the top of the doorframe.

I stifled a giggle. They were understandably curious. I would have been curious too if the situation had been reversed. But I was happy Penny was willing to speak with me.

Penny walked to the porch swing and sat. "How can I help you, Shelby?" She patted the seat next to her.

I was too antsy to sit. "I don't know what to do."

"Okay, with what?"

I sighed. "Things are a mess with my family. My parents both think I've changed and am acting counterproductively to our family's goals."

Penny stroked her chin. "I see. And how do you feel about the situation?"

"I think I'm doing what's right."

"Mm-hmm. May I ask what the situation is?"

"You promise to not get upset?"

"I can do my best."

"Okay." I took a deep breath. "They aren't happy with my connection to Riley and Randy. I don't think it should matter what their parents did or haven't done. It shouldn't be held against them in our community." I walked to the swing and sat. "I had to give a proposal at the founders council meeting. It was supposed to be just me, but Mr. Walker proposed that Randy could help me. My father wasn't happy with the idea, but I told him I would hear him out and then not use him for the proposal. It was supposed to be easy, but then I heard his ideas, and they were good. I didn't want to cut him from the project if we chose to go with his plan."

Penny watched me silently.

"We gave our presentation today, and my father was furious with me that I allowed Randy to help and present. It's not his fault that his father fell apart. It's not fair."

"And why do they feel like you should distance yourself from them?"

I rolled my eyes. "They are so focused on our image and who we spend time with. My mom always says, 'We are who we associate with, Shelby.' She doesn't think that who I associate with is appropriate anymore."

"Who do you think you should associate with?"

"I want the freedom to find real friends. Tabitha and Priscilla are shoved down my throat, but they aren't genuine. They would do the same thing to me that they did to Riley." I cringed remembering what my mother had told me. "In fact, my mother orchestrated that. She told me today. I can't believe she gave Tabitha and Priscilla information about Riley's mom just to affect the relationship I was trying to build with her."

Penny's nose scrunched. "While I don't approve of the results, I do know parents tend to do things they think are right for their children. Is it possible your mother was trying to protect you from danger she thought would happen?"

I shrugged. "I have no idea. How could Riley be danger-ous? Or even Randy, for that matter?"

"I'm not sure I'm the best to know that"—she smiled and patted my leg—"considering I'm on the wrong side of this equation. But I can imagine your parents are concerned for your future. They think they are protecting you the best way they can."

"But they crush who I am in the same instance. Even if I entered dangerous positions, I would learn from it. Can't they see they are dismissing who I am? And I think I could become stronger if I had real friends, people I knew weren't using me." I lay my head in my hands. "That's all I'm good for —their image and doing whatever is necessary to improve their clout. I just want to be me."

"I'm sorry. I don't have all the answers. Is there a way to have this conversation with them?"

"I don't know, but I don't think so."

"Well, I think if you told them why you want to, it couldn't hurt—if there was a way to get them to listen to you."

"You don't know what they'd do. My mother already threatened me if I didn't get my act together. Confessing that I want to go against everything they have taught me might come off with the opposite reaction."

"Hmm. Well, all you can do is try. Maybe take baby steps? Do something for them to show you still love them and that you won't go against who they are, but that you need to make changes for you."

"Maybe." I had strong doubts, but I wasn't sure I knew what else to do.

Penny stood. "Do you want to come in and have some sweet tea? I can make a fresh batch."

I shook my head. "I should probably head home. I didn't ask to leave, and I don't want them to notice I'm gone." I turned to walk away but stopped. "Thank you for listening to me. I really appreciate that."

Penny smiled. "I'm always here to listen to someone trying to better their lives. If you ever need anything, just let me know."

"I definitely will. Bye, Mrs. Brooks."

"The name's Penny. And don't be a stranger."

I waved and returned to my aunt's rental. My chest felt a little lighter, but I had absolutely no idea how I would have a heart to heart with my parents and get them to listen to me. That seemed nearly impossible.

~

When I had finally made it home, no one was around, which was fine by me. I trudged to the kitchen to find Chef Frank.

He was wiping down the counters and the stove as I entered. "Hello, Miss Shelby. Can I get you something?"

"Got anything for a bad day?"

He rubbed his chin then snapped his fingers. "I have something in mind. Have a seat in the entertainment room. I'll bring it to you."

"Thanks, Chef Frank."

He winked. "Anything for you."

I smiled and did as he had asked. He really was the best chef we had ever had. I plopped on the sofa and scrolled on my phone. Nothing was very interesting, until a text from Luke popped up on my screen.

Congratulations on your proposal. My dad said you and Randy did a great job.

Thanks. I'm glad he liked it.

That doesn't sound very exciting. You should be joyous. I'm sure your dad was proud of you!

Not really.

What? Why?

Long story.

I have time.

I smiled. Did he really want to hear how my day had gone? Or was this still a ploy? I shook my head. If I didn't take a chance, how would I ever find out?

My father was furious with me. Randy wasn't supposed to come anywhere near the proposal, and he wasn't glowing when he stood up and presented it with me. He stood by it in the meeting, but he practically screamed at me in the car and when we got home.

I'm so sorry, Shelby. That seems ridiculous. You'll be doing *something important for the town. He should appreciate that.*

You would think, but, like I said, who I do that with matters to them. Then my mother made it worse.

Oh?

She told me that an incident from school was her handiwork. She gave the ammo to Tabitha and Priscilla to pull it off. It makes me sick.

I'm sorry. I hope you find a way to celebrate anyway.

It is what it is. My chef is making me something. But thanks for listening.

No problem. That's what friends are for ... That is, as long as we are friends?

I laughed. Why was it so important to him that I said yes? *Okay. Yes, we can be friends.*

Wahooo!

I giggled.

"What's funny?" Chef Frank asked as he carried a platter to me.

I startled. "Oh nothing. What did you bring me?"

"The perfect cure for a bad day—a huge ice cream sundae, hot chocolate with peppermint candy canes, and you're favorite, mac n' cheese."

I beamed. "You seriously are the best!"

"I know. Enjoy!"

He walked away and left me alone to eat my feelings. All in all, it was quite satisfying.

$\mathcal{M}$y punishment from my parents was the silent treatment. For the past three days, my parents ignored me when we all were in the same room. I should have expected it—it was their favorite punishment—but it still didn't make it feel any better.

I stared from my bedroom window, moping when my phone chirped. I swiped the screen to unlock and check the notification.

It was a message from Luke. *Hey, what're you up to?*

I smiled and texted back, *Nothing. Sitting in my room.*

Yawn! It's New Year's Eve. You can't spend it alone.

I'm still in the doghouse with my parents. Plus, we never do anything tonight.

What? Well, get ready. I'll come pick you up.

I don't know. My parents are still pretty mad.

That's easy. I'm a Warrington. Don't worry about it. Just get dressed.

Okay. How long until you pick me up?

Thirty minutes.

What? I was screwed. I stared at my pajama bottoms and

screeched. There was absolutely no way I would make it in thirty minutes. I scurried to the bathroom and checked my reflection in the mirror. My dark hair resembled a rat's nest on the top of my head. I grabbed my brush and combed it out. Then I used a volumizer to add some lift. I grabbed my curling iron, plugged it in and ran to the closet.

I stared at the clothes, trying to decide what was the best to wear. I didn't want to be overdressed or underdressed. I rubbed the materials between my fingers as I floated down the length of my closet. I settled on a light purple cashmere sweater. I paired it with dark-wash jeans and my favorite brown knee-high boots.

Once I was dressed, I ran back to the bathroom. The curling iron was just the perfect temperature. I sectioned my hair and curled each strand. The hairspray held it together, then I looked at my face. There wasn't enough time to do anything crazy, so I settled on eyeliner, mascara, my favorite eye shadow, and lip gloss. Just as I put away my makeup and curling iron, my phone chirped. I snatched it off my bed and unlocked it.

Luke had sent another message. *Be there in five minutes.*

Perfect timing. I checked my reflection one more time and swished my hair to watch the curls bounce effortlessly. I crept from my room and down the hallway to the stairs. Just as I began to descend, the doorbell rang. *Rats!* I wanted to sneak out before my parents had time to process it.

The sound of heels clacking against the floor emanated up the foyer walls.

I took the stairs faster to meet her at the door.

My mother eyed me warily before she answered.

Luke smiled as she opened the door. He looked dashing. His green collared shirt poked out the top of his tan sweater. He wore dark-wash jeans and a navy-blue coat.

Wow. Did he always seem this handsome?

"Luke. Were we expecting you?" my mother asked.

I moved ahead of her and smiled at Luke. "I was."

Luke entered our foyer and hugged my mother.

She tensed but allowed the hug. "Oh?"

"I asked Shelby if she would join me at my parents' house for New Year's Eve."

My mother pursed her lips and looked between us.

"My mother and father are looking forward to getting to know Shelby better."

Her face slackened ever so slightly. "Well, I suppose that would be a good thing."

"And don't worry, I'll have her back after the ball drops."

"I … uh."

I could tell Mother was caught. She didn't want to irritate another family, especially not a founding family, but I knew she wasn't thrilled with the idea of letting me have fun when I should have been stewing in my room all alone.

She straightened and adjusted her dress. "That will be fine."

I shot Luke a thumbs-up from behind her.

Luke beamed. "Thank you, Mrs. Rowe."

"Yes, well, make sure you don't stay out too late, Shelby."

I averted my gaze to the floor. "I won't. Thank you." I kissed her on the cheek, bolted to the closet to grab my coat and nearly sprinted from the front door.

Once the door shut and I heard it click, I ran to Luke and hugged him. "You sprung me! Thank you."

Luke chuckled. "You didn't look to be imprisoned to me."

"Oh, I was. Practically in the dungeons."

Luke rolled his eyes and walked around to the side of his hunter-green Audi. He opened the door, and I scooted onto the seat. Once I buckled, he walked around and got in.

"Is it warm enough?" he asked as he fiddled with the thermostat controllers.

"Yeah, I'm good. Thank you." I played with my coat's zipper. "Am I really meeting your parents?"

"Nah. They went to the mountains to ski. Won't be back until after I leave for school."

My eyes widened. "So, we'll be alone at your house?"

He nodded.

"What if my parents find out? Or ask your parents about it at a meeting."

He shrugged. "I doubt anyone would do that, and, if they did, my parents would lie, especially my dad. Can't show weakness. If he doesn't remember, he just wings it."

"Maybe."

Luke chuckled. "It'll be fine. Don't worry so much."

I attempted to smile, but it fell short. "I just don't need to get in anymore trouble."

Luke's right eyebrow rose above the other. "They are still that mad?"

"Yep."

"That's crazy to me. It's a sound business venture."

"But it was done with Randy Walker."

Luke eyed me then stared back at the road. "And?"

My brows knitted together. "Isn't the Walker family on the outs in the council?"

Luke shrugged. "I guess to a special few. But most understand they're going through a hard time—a lot of families are."

I turned in the seat to face him more. "So, your father didn't see anything wrong with Randy being a part of the proposal?"

Luke shook his head.

"Hmm. Well, that's good to know."

"I'm sorry your father is going to this extreme. It seems childish."

"Yep, but honestly, my mother was worse, accusing me of

not doing what was best for our family." I shook my head. "I swear I can't please them. They should have made a robot daughter and coded her to do what they wanted. They don't want me to think unless it makes a difference to them. If I go against the grain, I'm dishonoring them all." I sighed and faced the window. Luke should have run far away from me. All I would do is ruin the evening.

Luke's hand enclosed around mine. "Don't doubt what makes you who you are. They'll come around. Either that or they're idiots."

I smiled. "Thanks, but they don't make it easy. It's all too much pressure."

He squeezed my hand. "Well, let's forget about them. Release all that pressure and all those obligations. Just be you tonight." He smirked. "I'll make sure not to tell everyone how soft you really are."

I narrowed my gaze. "Oh, think you're funny, do you?" I pinched his finger.

"Ow!" he howled.

I giggled.

He smiled then made his face serious. "Hmm. I'll remember that."

I stuck out my tongue.

"But seriously. Ignore what they said. They don't know everything, and, as I've heard it, you deserve to have a rockin' New Year's Eve."

"Thank you."

Luke kept surprising me. I had pegged him so differently before. Once again, I acted just as badly as my parents had by judging someone by their name before I knew them.

I didn't usually believe in New Year's resolutions, but, if I had to choose one, it would be to stop judging people before I really knew them. No matter their name or appearance, I would give them a chance. If I ever expected to have real friends, I needed to stop doing that. Otherwise, I would never make any.

We pulled into a large driveway with an entrance gate. Luke reached for the remote on his visor, and the gate before us opened.

I had never been at the Warrington Estate. I peered out the window as I tried to catalog it all. Some sort of trees lined the drive. In all directions was ground that just kept going. After a minute or so, we reached a circle in the driveway. On the right at the first stop was a large four-car garage.

He clicked the second remote on the visor, and the door opened. He pulled in and exited the car.

As I waited for him to walk around, I surveyed the rest of the garage. One spot was empty; the others contained vehicles underneath covers. My door opened, and Luke proffered his hand. I took it gladly. The warmth from his fingers seeped into my chilly hand.

"Wow! Your hands are cold. You should have said something. I would have turned up the heat."

My cheeks felt warm, like after drinking hot cocoa. "It's okay. I'm used to it."

He took his other hand and held it over my hand as he sandwiched in-between both of his. The warmth oozed into my body and caused me to shiver.

Our eyes met as he held my hand. The light accentuated the flecks of blond in his brown hair.

I pulled my hand away and looked down.

Luke stared a moment longer then padded his pockets. He shut the passenger door and locked the car.

I followed him into a side door. It opened into a hallway with family photos strewn all the way down. I moved closer and stared at the family within the frames. They looked so happy.

"Oh, man. I should have gone the other way. You don't want to see those."

"Yes, I do."

He shuffled me forward as I resisted. I tried to stare at them all, but there was just too many.

The end of the hallway opened into a large kitchen—marble countertops and white shaker cabinets.

"Wow. This is gorgeous."

"My mother loves to cook. It was my father's Christmas present to her a few years back. They redid the whole thing."

We walked by the large island and down another hallway. Luke took the first right door and opened it, allowing me to go first.

My eyes adjusted to the dark while Luke turned on the light. It was a theater room.

"You have a theater in your house? That's awesome."

"You don't have one?"

"Of course not. My parents don't believe in such frivolity."

Luke grasped his chest. "Ouch! I'm wounded."

I giggled. "I didn't say I didn't believe in it. I would love to have a theater inside the house."

Luke plopped into one of the lounge chairs. "Yeah, it's nice, especially for nights like tonight. I can pull up any TV channel and watch the ball drop."

I took a seat next to him. "No partying for you? But you go back to school soon."

"No parties. You must know people here to have a party, and yeah, I go back soon, so what?"

"You know people here."

Luke shook his head. "Not like you do. Going to an Ivy league preparatory school out of town doesn't lend itself to nearby friends."

"I guess that's true."

I never thought how lonely it must be to attend school out of state, never seeing your friends on holidays and having fun. "I doubt the town would mind if you invited everyone our age, whether they knew you or not."

Luke chuckled. "That may be true, but it's not my scene."

I gasped. "You don't like the party scene?"

"Not if I have to be the center of attention."

"Really?"

He nodded.

"I would have never guessed you didn't like the attention."

He smirked. "There's a lot about me you don't know."

"Oh? Like what?"

"For instance, I took dance lessons when I was younger. I can't be expected to woo all the beautiful women at dances if I didn't."

I smirked. "And?"

"I have a love of sloths. I have no idea why, but they are secretly my most cherished animal."

"No way. You're making it up."

He crossed his heart. "On my honor, I swear."

"So, you took dance lessons and love sloths. Anything else?"

He stroked his chin. "Hmm. I despise sodas. Strictly water for me. And ..." He looked away. "My favorite movie genre is romantic comedies."

I gasped and burst into a fit of giggles. "No way. There's absolutely no possible way I believe any of that."

Luke knitted his brows. "Why's that?"

"It's like the *exact* opposite of everything I picture about you."

Luke's eyebrow rose. "You picture me?" He wiggled his brows up and down. "How scandalous."

I playfully slapped his arm. "Cut it out. You know what I

mean. Everything I pegged you to enjoy or like is wrong. Horribly wrong in fact."

Luke chuckled. "Yeah, it happens. Most people don't really get to know me. They see the last name Warrington and expect to know everything just from my name."

"I know how that goes. It's like this invisible barrier that prevents anything from getting through. No matter what I say, I can't be genuine or true if I'm a Rowe."

"Then make them. I gave up on trying to fix people's view of me. If they want to peg me as an arrogant, stuck-up prick because my family has money and I'm an only child, let them. If they want to get to know the real me, they will try and be interested in my life." He tousled his hair. "You know, they actually do me a favor. I know who to make an effort with based on how they react to my name. If they treat me like a normal human being, I know they are a cool person to get to know. They save me from the imposters who wish to mingle with a Warrington."

"That's all true, but it's also incredibly lonely and defeating. If no one makes the effort, how do you ever have someone you can trust or be around?"

He nudged my arm. "I'm here, aren't I?"

I giggled. "Fair enough. Although …" I grabbed a pillow and hid my face. "I *may* have been one of those people to peg you for something you aren't."

"I'll give you a pass. On one condition."

I peeked over the top of the pillow. "What's that?"

"We watch a movie, and you don't laugh at whatever I choose."

I extended my hand. "Done deal, good sir."

He chuckled and squeezed my hand. "But to be honest, I had the same issue. So, we're even. Having parents force you to do things kind of makes it hard to trust whoever is pushed in your direction."

"Exactly! And with my parents anyway, if they like something, it tends to be too good to be true."

Luke raised an eyebrow. "Is that so? I'm too good to be true, huh?"

I stammered. "That's not what I meant ..."

"I'm only kidding, Shelby. You've been forgiven of your former follies and misconceptions. We can have a fresh start."

I smiled. "Perfect."

Luke stood and grabbed a remote. When he sat, he reclined his lounger until he was almost completely horizontal. He snagged a pillow to raise his head so he could see.

I stared at him as he lounged back and flipped through options on the screen. Was I really about to watch a movie with Luke Warrington? Alone? If someone had told me it was possible, I would have told them they were crazy. There was absolutely no way I would have even contemplated this, let alone noticed how his hair fell just over his right eye and how whiffs of his cologne infiltrated my senses when he moved too fast.

Wait, what? What was I saying? I couldn't like Luke Warrington. That would be the absolute worst thing. My mother would think she won. She would think she actually did something right and be pretentious and smug the entire time she was informing me of her win.

But ... he was also super cute. And he understood my family dynamics better than most. Could things ever be genuine between us? Could something happen?

Luke nudged my arm. "You okay? Your face got all scrunchy and serious."

"What? It did not."

"Did too. What were you thinking about?"

Flames licked at my cheeks. I couldn't admit anything to him.

"Oh, it must be good. Your cheeks could outdo Rudolph's red nose."

My hands flew to my cheeks. I patted them as if that would make the embarrassment lessen. "I was thinking about my parents."

Luke eyed me warily. "Mm-hmm. Sure ya were." He put his lounger into the upright position. "Anyway, I was trying to ask if you wanted popcorn. But you couldn't hear me, I suppose."

"Oh. Sorry, yeah sure." I eyed him carefully. "You don't have any movie theater popcorn maker hiding anywhere, do you?"

He chuckled. "Of course not. Is the microwave kind fine?"

I nodded.

He walked from the room and left me alone. Some movie title displayed prominently on the screen. Whatever he picked, I would put money on the fact it was a romantic comedy. At least I hadn't seen it before; although that was easy to do, considering I rarely saw movies. My life was too busy to sit and watch movies or TV. Occasionally, I was allowed to attend the movies with Priscilla and Tabitha, but it took major convincing on my part to get my mother to agree.

While I waited, I shrugged off my coat and set it on the chair next to me. I grabbed my phone and checked the notifications. I had nothing, not even a text message. I shoved the phone into my coat pocket and made myself comfortable. Just as I lowered the lounger into the perfect angle, Luke carried in a large bowl of popcorn.

"I hope you don't mind if we share."

"Not at all," I said.

～

*T*he ending credits rolled up the screen, and Luke fixed the lights. The movie was cute—classic guy meets girl and they end up together, with lots of funny obstacles in-between. But what was better was watching it with Luke. There was no awkwardness. No attempts at things he shouldn't. He stayed true to his word and watched the movie. Our fingers brushed here or there while getting popcorn, but nothing happened, and I was thankful. It was one thing to be curious about what might happen and another to be ready for him to make a move.

Luke stretched in front of his chair. "That was a good movie. Wasn't too corny for you, was it?"

"No. Every genre has a time and place. This was a good choice."

Luke smiled. "I'm glad." He pulled his phone from his pocket. "Only a half hour until midnight. Are you ready to start a new year?"

"Ready? Probably not the word I would pick, but it's coming whether we want it to or not. So, I'll take whatever it throws at me."

"That's the spirit!"

I giggled. "If you say so."

Luke changed the input to the projector screen and chose a live cable broadcast instead. The countdown to midnight rolled in the banner at the bottom of the screen. "I absolutely do."

I stood. "Do you have a bathroom nearby?"

"Of course. Let me show you." Luke led me into the hallway and continued farther to his right. He stopped at the first door on the left and opened the door, leaving it ajar.

"Thank you."

Once inside, I quietly closed the door and flipped on the light. The walls were a mint color with coral accents for hand towels and rugs. It was a half bath, but it was still massive. I could easily lay on the floor twice and still have room before I touched the door. I checked my reflection in the mirror; my curls were still set, and my makeup wasn't affected from the popcorn. I finished using the bathroom and returned to the theater.

Luke sat in the lounge chair, watching the TV. He smiled when I returned. "Getting closer!"

"Yep, it is."

"Do you make resolutions?"

I shook my head. "Not usually."

"But …?"

"I considered making one this year."

"Ooh. Interesting. Care to share?"

"Nothing crazy. Just to work on myself more, be a better person—that kind of thing." I narrowed my eyes. "What about you?"

"I don't do them."

"What? That's not fair. I shared, so you must as well."

He shook his head. "Nope."

I crossed my arms. "Pfft. Figures."

He chuckled. "I've never made them. Why make them specifically one night a year? Why not resolve to be better and do better always? Otherwise, it seems to be temporary, and I don't want that."

I thought about all the resolutions I knew people made, and he had a point. Most people stopped working on themselves after the first two weeks of January. "I suppose."

He wiggled his eyebrows. "You know I'm right."

I crossed my arms. "I admit to nothing."

He laughed. "You're so stubborn."

We watched the screen as the countdown got closer to midnight.

"Are you looking forward to going back to school?"

"Yes and no. It's school, so that's okay, I guess. But it sucks to be away from home so much. I wish I could have just gone to Honey Cove High, but my parents never wanted to listen."

"I understand. If it helps, going back to school doesn't sound too appealing to me either right now. I can't avoid certain people as well, and I don't want to deal with it right now."

"So, change who you hang out with. It's obvious to me you don't care for Tabitha and Priscilla. So, why torture yourself?"

"Because, what if my mother makes my life miserable?"

"Isn't she already? What would be the difference?"

I contemplated what he said. I did feel miserable having to deal with them and be the person she expected. What if I could get away from them? Spend time with Riley or Randy. How much worse could it really get?

"Maybe. They're still my parents, you know? I want them to be proud of me still."

Luke smiled sweetly. "They'd be crazy not to be proud of you."

I averted my gaze. "Thanks. That's nice to say, even if I don't always believe it."

The broadcast got louder as the counter struck two minutes left until midnight. The crowds roared and clapped as the final performance ended.

Sixty seconds left.

Luke stared at me.

Fifty seconds.

I watched his face contort into a devilish grin.

Forty seconds.

He took my hand in his as he stroked my thumb with his thumb.

My stomach dropped like going over the large hill on a roller coaster.

Thirty seconds.

I stared at the screen, trying to avoid the heat that crawled up my cheeks as he stared at the side of my face.

Twenty seconds.

He broke his gaze to look at the screen but snuck sideways glances at me. What was he planning to do?

Ten seconds.

He dropped our hands and stood.

Five seconds.

He pulled me to my feet, and I looked up into his eyes.

The screen shouted, "Happy New Years!"

Luke leaned closer and embraced me. He kissed the top of my head. He held us together for a few more seconds then let go. "I should drive you home."

I kept my head down as I relived the feeling of his arms around me. He had held me tenderly, and the kiss to my head, while it hadn't made my toes curl, had wrapped my heart in a hug—so sweet and gentle.

I shrugged on my coat and watched as Luke grabbed our popcorn bowl and turned off the projector. We walked through the doorway, and he dropped off the bowl. He found his coat and returned to open the door for me, and a blast of cold air blew through.

I shivered and stared through the doorway to the little white flakes falling from the sky. I stepped outside and leaned my head backward, letting the flakes fall on my face.

"Wow. Haven't seen snow this early in a while," Luke said.

"Me neither, but I love it." I righted my head and stared at Luke while he waited by the door of his Audi.

Tonight had turned out to be absolutely perfect. What did I say to thank him for rescuing me from a mediocre night full of self-loathing? I shivered again.

"We should get in. You'll freeze out here."

I smiled and walked to the door and got in. I could have

stayed out there all night, but he was right; I hadn't dressed to endure a snowstorm.

Luke got in with me and turned on his windshield wipers to knock off the loose snow. The Audi wasn't covered with snow, so it must have just started falling, but it was still beautiful.

I loved to watch the delicate little flakes float down and disappear as they touched the ground.

"Don't worry, I'll go easy to your house," Luke said as he strained to look through the window at the blustering snowfall as we left his driveway.

"I'm not worried. I trust you."

Luke feigned shock. "You trust me? Woah, we've grown, haven't we?"

I rolled my eyes. "I trust you *to drive.*"

"Ah, just to drive?"

I shrugged. "For now."

He poked me in the side. "You don't fool me, Shelby Rowe. You have an ooey-gooey center."

I arched my eyebrow and turned to face him "I do, do I?"

He nodded. "Can't fool me."

I giggled. I turned and looked out the window as the greenery flew by, with the speckle of white blurred with it. "How long until you return home from school?"

Luke glanced in my direction then refocused on the road. "Technically, I can come home any weekend I want, but I'm usually stuck there until the next holiday break."

I twisted my sweater in my hands. "Oh. So that would be Easter?"

"I think so."

"Gotcha."

Luke eyed me warily. "Is someone going to miss me?"

I crossed my arms. "Absolutely not. I just needed to know when to expect you to invade town again."

Luke chuckled. "Prickliness won't work on me anymore. I've seen your softer side. It's okay to miss me." He took his eyes off the road and stared at me until I turned. "I'll miss you."

My jaw slackened. "You will?"

"Of course, Shelby. I don't invite everyone to my house to hang out. I like getting to know you. The *real* you."

I smiled. How had the boy I had considered an arrogant prick turn into such a gentleman? I wouldn't admit it, but I had enjoyed getting to know him too. Things were nice how they were. I could only hope we would stay friends when he returned to school. I couldn't take anymore setbacks with real friends.

CHAPTER 18

J lay in bed and relived every moment of New Year's Eve. Luke had been a gentleman the entire night. His kiss at midnight was the sweetest thing I had experienced in my entire life. When he dropped me off, the snow had stopped but not before depositing an inch. He walked me to the front door and hugged me one final time before I watched him drive away in his Audi.

We made no promises about his time at school. I didn't know if we would talk, and I found myself more disappointed than I had thought would be possible.

A light knock wrapped on the door. "Shelby?"

"Come in!"

Aunt Delilah peeked through the doorway then skipped to my bed until she plopped down. "Happy New Year!"

I smiled. "Happy New Year! Did you do anything fun?"

"Nah, I'm too old for that."

"No, you aren't."

My aunt giggled. "What did you do? I came in around midnight to see if you were up, and you weren't in your room."

"I went to Luke's last night."

My aunt winked at me. "Oh?"

I rolled my eyes. "Nothing happened. We watched a movie."

"Interesting."

I crossed my arms. "Why is that interesting?"

"No reason. You just detested him a few days ago."

"Detest is a strong word."

My aunt raised her eyebrow. "Since when?"

I shrugged. "I don't know. I found him annoying, but I didn't detest him."

"Someone's in denial."

My eyebrows knitted together. "I'm not in denial, Aunt Delilah."

"Whatever you say." She eyed my outfit. "Are you still in PJs? Your mother will kill you if she comes up here."

"She won't come up here. I'm still in trouble."

"Well, I'm sure you still have to eat. Get dressed and come downstairs with me. I'm starving."

"Okay, but only for you."

She smirked and slunk out of my bedroom.

I walked to my closet and stared at my options. I settled on black leggings and my favorite green sweater dress. It would be the right amount of comfy and stylish to please my mother if I saw her. I took the front stairs and tiptoed down in my socks.

My aunt sat at the dining room table by herself scrolling on her phone.

I scanned the room and breathed a sigh of relief when no one else lurked around the room. At least for now I could avoid my parents.

"Whatcha going to eat today?" I asked.

"I was thinking French toast. What about you?"

"That sounds good."

"Perfect."

I buzzed the call button for chef Frank.

He entered the dining room. "What can I make you both?"

"Cinnamon French toast please," Delilah said.

"Oh, and bacon!" I added.

He nodded and went to the stove.

"So how long are you staying with us? Do you have to go home now that the holidays are over?"

Delilah shook her head. "Nope. I'm here for a while longer."

I smiled. "I'm glad. It's nice having you around. I can't imagine how much lonelier it would be if it was just us."

"You'd work it out, I'm sure."

I shook my head. "I don't know. This is our worst blow up we've had. Not to mention the fact they seem to be upset as well."

My aunt averted her gaze. "It'll be fine, I'm sure."

I scrunched my nose. "What's up with you? You're never on their side."

She shrugged. "Nothing. Just sometimes things are more complicated than they appear."

"If you say so." I stared at her while she focused on her phone.

Frank brought our breakfast.

I stabbed the French toast with my fork and pushed it around the syrup. I couldn't shake the feeling I had missed something massively important about the adults in my life. None of them made any sense anymore.

~

*A*unt Delilah bolted from the table when breakfast was over. She didn't even say goodbye. She avoided my gaze for the rest of breakfast then left me alone. I took both our plates to the kitchen sink and pushed in our chairs.

It was the last day before break ended, and I had no idea what else to do with myself. I meandered down the hallway toward the office-library at the back of the house. It remained mostly vacated, unless my father was in his office and my mother happened to need a quiet place.

I opened the door and listened to it creak as it was forced to let me in. Bookshelves lined the walls. At the center of the back wall was a large desk, and in front were two large-backed armchairs. I lingered by the first bookshelf and scanned the titles. Nothing spoke to me, so I moved to the next shelf.

A large cough emitted from the back of the room. My father stood at the doorway.

"Can I help you with something?" I asked.

"Looking for a book?"

I nodded.

"You could try the fourth shelf. I added a few mystery books from my travels."

"Yeah, maybe."

He moved closer. I could feel him standing behind me. "Can we talk, Shelby?"

I turned and faced him. "Of course." I lied, but I wasn't allowed to deny any of his wishes, even if it was the last thing I wanted to do.

"Can we talk about the other day?"

I tucked a strand of hair behind my ear. "Sure."

He tapped the chair and sat in the other one across from it.

I sat and fiddled with my dress.

"I think we need to have a more productive conversation about the proposal."

I sat up straight. "Okay."

"I was upset because I wanted the attention to focus on you. Many of those men are old-fashioned. They have made comments for having you even in the meetings. I wanted them to see you could stand on your own and make them eat crow."

"I understand that."

"The Walkers don't have the best reputation right now. And I didn't want that to add to their view of you. The proposal was very good, but it makes it harder for some of those families to see what you're capable of, especially since you had Randy's help too. Reputation is everything in that room."

"I understand that, but I want our reputation to be based on how efficient, productive, and successful we are. If we are dismissing others or belittling them to get there, I don't know that I want *my* reputation to be based that way anymore."

"There's a tough line in this world, Shelby. Sometimes you have to step on a few toes to get where you want."

"Not if those toes are people who don't deserve it." I sighed. "I know I have a lot of work cut out for me with those stuffy old men in that council, but Randy is part of the future of this town too, whether you or those other men like it. He deserves a chance to show what he can do just as much as I do. If I didn't think he knew what he was discussing I wouldn't have listened."

"I suppose I see what you're saying. But it isn't always so black and white, Shelby."

"No, but this situation was. And so was the situation about Riley with Mother. If we have all this power and we refuse to do any good with it, what is it worth?"

My father's face scrunched. "We are doing good, Shelby. We provide jobs for so many in this town. We run charities—"

I raised my hand. "None of that requires us to do much. We show up, and we leave. What about doing what's right, even if we must get down in the mud?"

He shook his head. "You're being stubborn about this. But even in your analogy, you must be ready to get the mud on you. Are you ready for what that looks like?"

I shrugged. "If at the end of the day I'm doing what's right, then so be it. I think it's time we open up the council to more than just the thoughts of the founders." I stood and waited for my father to do the same. I wanted to walk out, but I knew it wasn't polite, even if we had just been arguing.

He stood and grabbed a paperback novel from the bookshelf and handed it to me. "I think you'd like it." Then he left the room.

I stared at the cover as I twisted it in my hands. My father seemed a tad more understanding today, but he still didn't see what I meant. I supposed he had experienced things with these same people and that he probably did generally know what he was talking about, but the more I thought about it, the less I could sacrifice being a decent human being just to please them.

CHAPTER 19

*I*t was the first day of school in a new calendar year, and all I wanted to do was to crawl under the covers and hide. Unfortunately, that would have been impossible to get away with. So instead, I got dressed and drove to school. The hallways were abuzz with chatter of exciting Christmas breaks and vacations.

I practically bolted to my locker. Classes would be a welcome distraction—something I never imagined I would say. I took a shortcut to my first class to avoid Tabitha and Priscilla. While we didn't have the exact same schedule, our classes weren't far from each other. And, at this point, I wanted nothing more than to be as far away from them both as possible.

I took my seat and forced my brain and ears to focus. Only three hours until lunch then the real crazy would begin.

*L*unchtime came faster than I expected. I stood in the entryway of the cafeteria and focused on my empty lunch table. I could sit there and be joined by Tabitha and Priscilla, or I could choose a different table entirely. People would talk about it surely, but the question was, did I care at this point? No.

I veered to the left of my table toward three people in mid-conversation. I knew it could be risky, but I hoped they would be mostly welcoming.

Sophie Graham stared at me as I approached her table. Her nose scrunched in disgust. "What on earth are *you* doing here?"

Randy and Riley swiveled in their seats and stared.

I plopped next to the seat on Randy's left side. "I hoped I could eat here for lunch."

Sophie's eyes widened. "Why would you hope to do that?" She looked between Randy and Riley. "Did I miss something that would make her think that was okay?"

"I-I could leave if you don't want me to sit here."

Randy's face pleaded with Riley.

"It's fine," Riley said.

Sophie crossed her arms. "What did I miss? This wasn't fine last year. So, what's the deal now?"

"She's attempted to apologize, Sophie," Riley said. "And … well, my mom-mom said to give her a chance."

Sophie huffed. "She apologized? And why would your mom-mom say to give her a chance?"

I raised my hand. "If I can explain?"

Sophie tightened her arms over her chest and nodded.

"I am trying to figure out things. As hard as it is for you to believe, the expectations and obligations my parents thrust on me aren't always ones I want to agree to."

Sophie snorted. "Oh, how sad. You had to wear a pink purse instead of a blue one?"

I stared at Sophie. While I deserved some distrust, that was rude. "Actually, no. I must *date* certain people or do proposals alone. And going along with that isn't how I want to live my life." I took a deep breath. "They don't make it easy. As you know, they are both influential, so going against their wishes isn't just being a teenage rebel ignoring their parents, dying their hair purple and getting a piercing. It's much larger than that. My mother has ways to get what she wants and make me miserable at the same time."

I watched their faces. Randy focused on the food on his lunch tray. Riley averted her gaze when I looked at her. Sophie's expression soured, but it wasn't as menacing as before.

"I know you don't trust me, and after this past fall, I don't blame any of you for keeping me at a distance. I just thought sitting with you all would be a welcomed change. But, like I said, if you don't want me to, I won't impose on you either."

Sophie pushed her peas around the plate with her fork. "I guess it's fine. But I'm watching you, Shelby. I don't trust you at all, even if those two have for some reason given in."

I smiled. "Thank you." I focused on my lunch and stayed as quiet as I could be while they chatted.

Sophie eyed Randy and Riley warily. "What did you two do over break?"

Riley shrugged. "Went to the ball and hung out with my family."

Sophie rolled her eyes. "That's it?"

"Yep. What about you, Sophie?" Riley asked.

"Nothing. Nothing worth telling anyway. Caleb drove me nuts."

Riley giggled. "Aww, but he loves his big sister."

"Whatever. He could love me from a far."

Randy smirked. "How does that work exactly?"

Sophie crossed her arms. "I don't know, but I wish it did."

"Sophie, you're lucky. You have a sibling. It's just me when I'm home."

"So? The peace and quiet must be nice."

"Ha! Hardly quiet. Being alone means my mom and my mom-mom focus on me only. That's worse than little brother attention any day."

Sophie stroked her chin. "I don't know. Let's swap and see."

Randy chuckled.

The pang in my stomach startled me. Their banter was endearing. Their connection genuine. Not to mention, my break had been the furthest from any of those things, and the reality of that difference hurt more than anything else.

I spied my normal table to see Priscilla and Tabitha sitting prominently in the center of the table, glaring at me from their vantage point. *Uh oh, I was in trouble.* There was no way their stares would go unnoticed. But lunch ended, and I bolted to class before they could do or say anything.

~

School had been a success—at least in the sense of avoiding Tabitha and Priscilla all day. I managed to leave the hallways just as they rounded a corner. It wouldn't work forever, but at least for the first day of school it did. Anything else would have been too much for me to manage.

I took the long way home. The garage was empty when I parked. I grabbed my bookbag from the back seat and walked to the large family room. I plopped on the sofa, kicked off my shoes and tucked my feet under me. I had homework to work on and plenty of silence to focus.

The teachers hadn't piled on the work quite so much, but we had midterms at the end of the month, and I wanted to stay on top of my schoolwork. Things would pick up, and I didn't want to get behind. Rowes didn't get poor grades either.

After tackling my math homework, I needed a break, plus my phone called to me. I scrolled through my contacts and clicked on the name I wanted to talk to. I typed my text and hit Send. *Hey, Luke! How's your first day back?*

I reread my text. Was it too much? Should I have deleted the exclamation point? I laid my head in my hands. This was ridiculous. What was wrong with me?

My phone chirped.

It's okay. I'd rather know how you are.

A smile broke out over my face. *You do, do you?*

Of course. Everyone is all uppity here about their vacations and travels. How were your friends?

I understand that. I avoided them mostly. They glared at me from a different lunch table though. I'll have to deal with it eventually, but for now, I got away with it.

Maybe it won't be as bad as you think?

Unlikely, I'm afraid.

Well, that's on them. What are you up to?

Homework.

Yuck. Go have fun, do something else.

I giggled. *What do you expect me to do?*

The familiar clacking sound of my mother's heels made me startle. My phone almost fell from my hand, but I caught it. I hurried to stow it, but I was too late.

"Who are you talking to, Shelby?"

I looked around the room. "No one."

"I heard laughing. Are you saying I'm crazy?"

I shook my head. "I was texting, Mother. I read something funny."

Mother's lips pursed together. "Oh? And who wrote the funny line?"

"Luke."

Her features softened but only slightly. "You text Luke? Since when?"

I shrugged. "Recently."

She crossed her arms. "I see."

"Did you need something? I want to get back to my homework." I felt my phone vibrate with a new message; the layers of blankets had muffled the chirp sound.

"I wanted to ask you about New Year's Eve at Luke's house and ask you *why* you changed your lunch seat today."

My eyes widened. "You know about that?"

"Of course, I do, Shelby. I'm very well connected. Something you should understand and already know. Don't think I didn't notice you didn't answer the question."

"I … was trying out a new table."

My mother threw her arms into the air. "A new table? With Randy Walker and Riley Mills? Shelby, have you lost all of your senses?"

"No."

"Then what is this? I warned you that if you didn't pull it together, I would take care of it. Apparently, I need to. You were warned, Shelby. I hope it was worth it." She turned on her heels and exited the room.

Whatever she planned to do, it would not be good.

CHAPTER 20

Changing my lunch seat turned out to be the best thing for my sanity. Not dealing with Tabitha and Priscilla picking on and complaining about others and me allowed me to relax. I slowly merged into Riley, Randy, and Sophie's world. It elated me to see the progress with Riley; other than my mother's threat, things were looking up.

"I don't want to do anymore winter conditioning," Riley said.

"You'll lose your progress if you don't. Fall will come back faster than you think," Randy said.

Riley sighed. "I guess, but it's just boring being in the gym on a treadmill instead of outside. It doesn't even feel that cold outside yet."

Randy chuckled. "So, go for your walks *and* do the winter conditioning."

I smiled as I focused on my lunch. Their little bickering was cute, but I didn't want them to think I listened too much, or they might stop talking altogether.

"Ugh. Why do you have to be so convincing?"

Randy smiled. "I was born with it."

Riley rolled her eyes. "Yeah, okay."

I giggled.

Riley looked at me and blushed. "Sorry. I'm sure discussing conditioning is boring to you."

I shook my head. "I enjoy it, you too squabbling like an old married couple."

Riley's cheeks reddened. "We do not."

Randy chuckled.

It was true; they were so in sync with each other. They balanced each other. Could Luke and I ever be like that? *Wait, what?* Luke and me? Where did that come from? I shook my head to push away the thoughts just as Sophie joined the table.

As she sat next to me, she elbowed me hard in the ribs.

"Ow!" I said as I rubbed the spot. "What the heck was that for? Did you lose your balance?"

"No. You deserved it. How could you say those things?"

My eyebrows knitted, and my nose scrunched up. "What things? I'm seriously confused here."

Sophie glared at me. "Did you two check your phones yet?"

Riley and Randy shook their heads and scrambled for their phones.

"What am I checking?" Riley asked. "I don't have messages."

"Buzz app."

Riley's face contorted as she tapped her phone screen, then her hand flew to her mouth.

Randy looked between us all. "What the …? Shelby, care to explain?"

Sophie crossed her arms. "I told you she was a snake. You should have listened to me when I said she shouldn't sit here. Once a selfish debutant, always a selfish debutant."

I gasped. What had happened? I didn't say anything on

the Buzz app. My thoughts screeched to a halt. *Oh no, no, no.* My fingers flew over the screen until I had the app open. I scrolled until I caught a glimpse of what they referred to. My eyes had to be playing tricks on me. They had to, because there was no way I had typed those messages in the screenshot. Absolutely no way!

I read the message. At the top, the sender's name was blurred, but it clearly said Shelby with a heart. Below that was a screenshot of messages I was supposed to have had with someone else. But the more I read, the more ridiculous it sounded. I would have never said any of it. The messages started with me. *I'm so sick of them both.*

Who?

Like, Riley and Randy. They're totally insufferable.

Really? They seem nice.

No! They make me want to vomit every time I see them together.

That sounds a little harsh.

I will tell you they're perfect for each other. With her slutty mother and his drunkard father, their families are perfect for each other. Keeping their hot mess of a family together saves everyone else the headache.

Wow, Shelby. That's kind of harsh!

I don't even care. The more I sit with them the worse they are ... bleck!

Below the screenshot was the text, *Shelby sits with them at lunch, but look at what she really thinks! Two-faced much? How can you trust her with anything?*

The more I read the post, the angrier I became. I looked up to see Riley's hands shaking.

Randy whispered in her ear, and Sophie glared at me with more intensity than the surface of the sun.

Riley's eyes glazed over, and she couldn't stop staring at her phone.

Sophie poked me in the side. "I think it's time for you to leave. For good. We didn't ask for your drama. If you don't like us, then get going. No one is forcing you to sit here."

The anger bubbled under my skin. I shook from the intensity. I swiveled in the chair until I could see Tabitha and Priscilla at our normal table. Their smirks were evident even from this distance. They acted like petulant children, and I was done with it! I pushed out the chair so quickly it toppled. Riley startled, and I practically growled as I marched toward Tabitha and Priscilla. This was the last time they put them or me through the ringer on that godforsaken app.

My hands slammed on the table, making them both blink and scowl.

"Saw our post, did you?" Priscilla asked and then snickered.

Tabitha smirked as she crossed her arms.

"What game do you two think you're playing?"

Tabitha smiled. "Us? Why, what do you mean?"

I slammed my hands down again. This time they did startle. "I will not stand by while you pull some elementary level antics *again*."

"Elementary?" Priscilla raised her left eyebrow. "This is not elementary. We're simply reminding you of what side you should be on."

My gaze narrowed. "You listen very carefully. You will remove the post. You will stop this nonsense. And you will do it now. Or so help me."

"Why would we do that, Shelby? You don't have the power."

"Oh I don't? You don't think I have worse things on the both of you? Things that are *true*? You had to resort to lying to implement your plan." I flipped my hair and surveyed the surrounding tables. No one appeared to notice our disagreement. "And don't think I don't know my mother's involvement from before and this time."

Priscilla's eyes widened. "What are you talking about?"

I rolled my eyes. "You two are pathetic, do you know that? You can't even create plans on your own. You have to be little puppets. And what's worse is you listen to her as your puppet master and don't question it. What is she promising you? More Rowe adventures? More invitations to our events? You two *need* my family, but I don't need you. And my mother will drop you two faster than you can sneeze." I leaned in closer and lowered my voice. "If you thought you would *ever* get back in my good graces, you can rest assured I am done with you both. I will never sit with you again. I won't socialize with you. And I won't protect you anymore. You two are on your own. I hope you like the limelight, because it'll be shining directly on you both from now on."

"But—"

"No, Tabitha. I don't want to hear the excuses. You two thought my mother's plan would blackmail me back into submission? That I wouldn't tell them I never said it and that I would have to come back here?"

They both nodded.

"And that's why your plans don't work. Because, if you had been listening to anything I've said the last few months, you'd know that. I'm tired of being cruel to people, especially those who haven't earned it. So, you make your silly little schemes, but what will people think when they learn you're lying? Or better yet, what will they think when they learn about the stuff *you two* say about others?"

Their eyes widened.

"Exactly. You want to play dirty? You should make sure your opponent has no ammo against you." I stood and pushed in my chair. "Good luck with the rest of your pitiful high school experience. I no longer care to be a part of it." I turned and walked away.

The anger still exploded from every part of my being. At the end of the day, those two were harmless without the pushing from my mother. They didn't have the sense to think for themselves, but she did. And she wouldn't escape my wrath. Not this time. Not ever again.

When I set her straight, I would make it up to Riley and Randy. It wouldn't be like before. Not again.

CHAPTER 21

It took enormous self-restraint not to throw something for the rest of the day. As soon as the bell rang at the end of my final class, I practically sprinted outside to drive home. I needed to confront my mother before I lost the courage. Plus, the anger helped to fuel me. It was one thing for her to have done that to Riley in the fall, but to do something again dealing with them just because she didn't like me associating with them was not only ridiculous but absolutely infuriating.

I would be eighteen this year, and she constantly treated me like a child incapable of understanding our social situations. I never said I wouldn't go to balls or functions; I just wanted the freedom to choose my own date or associate with good genuine people who had done nothing to deserve otherwise.

I barreled through the front door and stomped around until I heard the clacking noise from the hallway. I met my mother before she reached the foyer. "What were you thinking?"

"Excuse me? You do not talk to your mother that way, young lady."

I crossed my arms. "Sorry for the inappropriate way to bring up betrayal."

She squinted. "You better remember who you're speaking to before you land yourself in major trouble."

I threw my hands in the air. "Go ahead, Mother! I get in trouble with you for breathing the wrong way." I balled my hands. "You are insufferable. You're so miserable with your life that you have to run mine, and when I don't follow it exactly, you lose your mind. I'm not some puppet, Mother. You didn't raise me to be weak."

"Would you care to enlighten me before you continue to berate me?"

"You know what you did. You threatened me that if I didn't straighten up you would take care of the situation. So, what, your plan worked the last time, so you figured you would call Priscilla and Tabitha again and tell them to post on our school's app to irritate me and disrupt things with Riley and Randy?"

"I told you to take care of it. You didn't, so I did."

"That's how you manage it? You make me look like a liar to our school? How does that help our Rowe name? Our legacy? If you slander me, you slander us. Isn't that what you've always told me? Or have you forgotten your own rules?"

How, after everything, could she remain so high and mighty? It was simply infuriating.

"*I* didn't say anything, if you want to get technical about it. I merely told Tabitha and Priscilla it was time they did something again. What they wrote was up to them. Besides, it's on a stupid app, Shelby. Your reputation isn't damaged, but it will be good for you to remember the control I have. I can make it worse. I can do worse to your *friends* until you have no choice but to do what I say."

"So, that's your plan? Blackmail your daughter into doing what you want?" I bit the corner of my lip. "What a class act you turned out to be. I didn't realize my mother was a manipulative witch."

"Shelby Elizabeth Rowe!" my mother screamed.

I turned on my heels and walked away.

"Get back here!" she shouted at my back.

I sprinted up the stairs and slammed my bedroom door. My body tensed, and I paced the floor. She was completely absurd. Had she really thought that would work on me? Control me into submission? I'm a Rowe, for crying out loud! They instilled strength, courage, and bravery in the face of adversity. If anything, they should know better. I wouldn't break so easily.

A loud knock emanated from my door.

"Go away, Mother. I don't want to see you."

"It's Aunt Delilah."

I stalked to the door and opened it then went to my bed. I snatched my pillow and hugged it to my chest. I needed to calm down before I had a stroke or gave myself a migraine. Too much exertion wasn't good for me.

"What was with the screaming downstairs?" she asked.

"My mother butted into my life again. She had Tabitha and Priscilla post nonsense about me saying things about Randy and Riley." I sighed. "Why does she always have to be like that?"

"What did she say exactly?"

"Tabitha and Priscilla doctored a screenshot that made it look like I had said Randy and Riley were the perfect couple because of their messed-up families."

Delilah's eyebrows rose. "Oh my."

"Exactly. I can't believe she would pull something like that again. Well, I can somewhat, but it's just frustrating that she did. Why can't she trust me that I know what I'm doing?"

"Maybe she thinks she has good intentions?"

I scrunched my face. "You agree with her?"

"No. I just mean parents do things with their children's best interests at heart. Maybe she thinks she's protecting you from something."

"What she thinks she's protecting me from is associating with people she doesn't see as socially appropriate, which is just code for being a snob and elitist. I'm tired of it."

Aunt Delilah sighed. "I-I kept something from you."

"Oh?"

"I told you I didn't know who she liked."

"Yeah? What's that have to do with this?

"Your mother liked Beau Mills."

I gasped. "As in Riley's father?"

"When those girls had said those things to her, he let it happen. Our family wasn't as far down on the totem pole as Joanna's, but when he went for her, Vivian lost her mind."

"So, this is about her parents. Literally about the fact he chose her and not Mother?"

"Kind of. I think it was more that he ended up with someone who wasn't in his league, and yet he let those girls say things to her in the same position."

"But she doesn't get to run my life because of some eighteen-year vendetta."

"I don't pretend to understand what she does, Shelby, but I can tell you experience has guided her ever since. She most likely is trying to keep you from avoiding embarrassment based on your social stature."

I scrunched my face. "That's totally crazy. She is ruining my reputation *by* green lighting Tabitha and Priscilla. How would that not cause embarrassment?"

"She has them target your friends, not you directly. Sure,

this last one was more intense, but she isn't causing social suicide for you. She's doing it in a controlled manner. She does nothing she can't control."

I folded my arms. "She's still an absolutely horrible person. She could have been a totally different person, and she made the wrong choices. She doesn't do anything sincere or generous. Nothing truly, generous."

Aunt Delilah raised her hands in front of her. "I'm not siding with her. I just don't think you understand everything she does. She isn't an ice queen."

"Since when?"

My aunt sighed. "I'm not just visiting here. Your mother is letting me live here until I get back on my feet."

"Back on your feet?"

"I lost my job … and, well, a relationship exploded in my face. So, I'm staying until I figure it out."

"People lose their jobs, and relationships end. That doesn't mean she isn't an ice queen."

"Shelby, I don't know why, but you've always put me on this pedestal. And I don't deserve it. I'm not a good person. Your mother is right when she says I fail at running my life."

"I'm still not hearing anything that makes you a bad person."

"I didn't just lose my job. I got fired because my relationship was with a client … a married client."

My eyebrows rose. "Oh?"

"It sounds awful, and I suppose it is. But he was generous and kind. I didn't know he was married until later, and I was stupid enough to believe him when he said he would leave his wife. I screwed up, and your mother still let me stay. My boss found out and fired me instantly. He wouldn't risk the reputation of the company just for me."

"I didn't know." I couldn't imagine Delilah doing all of those things.

"See? You don't know all the circumstances, so is it possible you don't know them with your mother either?"

I shook my head. "I think it's the other way around. She doesn't know Randy and Riley besides what she hears. And, so what, if people talk? Shouldn't we show the others in town tolerance? Especially when they didn't do anything, only their parents did? No one should be condemned for the choices of others ... even you. If someone does something bad, shouldn't they have the option to redeem themselves? And shouldn't their children not be held accountable for it? It's old-fashioned. I don't want to partake in that. Whether she was wronged or not, she doesn't get to punish their children for no reason."

Delilah shrugged. "I don't know what the best answer is. But I know your mother can be a decent person, deep down. Otherwise, I wouldn't come around at all."

"I don't know."

Things were too confusing. How would I figure out what to do? Too many people were too close to the subject to offer me advice—too many but one.

"I'm going to the stables. Maybe seeing Rio will help. I'll see you later, Aunt Delilah."

Delilah waved as she sat on my bed.

I walked out and closed the door behind me. I would go outside near the stables, but I wouldn't see my horse. I had other plans.

CHAPTER 22

The meadow behind our house and by the stables had the perfect haze from the setting sun. I hated that it got so much darker so fast in the winter. But no humidity and pale blue skies weren't too bad either.

I opened the gate and strode inside. The horses were in the stables feeding, but the view and the privacy were unrivaled. The ground squished under my feet from our recent snow and sleet mixture. The perfect log for sitting and contemplating life resided in the back of the meadow by the tree line. It would guarantee privacy, and until the sun fully set, it would still be warm enough outside not to make me shiver too terribly.

Because, let's be honest, I didn't want *anyone* to overhear my conversation. I found the contact I was searching for and clicked on his name. It rang as I held the phone to my ear.

"Shelby?" Luke's voice sounded husky, like he had just woken up.

"Hey. Did I bother you?"

"No. You're fine." He cleared his throat. "What's up?"

"Are you sure I'm not bothering you?"

He chuckled. "I was resting my eyes. Nothing to worry about though. I'm glad you called."

I smiled. "How's the first week back?"

"The same."

"Very specific."

"It's just a means to an end. I find things to enjoy when they happen, but it's by no means my first choice. I manage. How'd things progress for you?"

"Not great. They became exponentially worse."

"How so?"

"Well, I sat with Riley and Randy for several days. My mother found out and had Tabitha and Priscilla post something on our school's app for the students. Basically saying I think Riley and Randy are a perfect couple because their families are both so messed up."

"Ouch."

"Yeah. So now I have to figure out how to navigate everything." I sighed. "Is it worth going against my mother, Luke? You know how our families are. I don't want to be in this constant struggle between them. I'm not disobeying our legacy; I'm trying to make my part in it."

"I don't know, Shelby. My parents don't seem as extreme. Sure, I have the boarding school and our arrangement for the ball, but my parents give me more freedom, I suppose."

"You're a guy, so you don't have to deal with your mother wanting you to be a debutant, marry well, and take care of a husband, house, and children. She has this deranged view that if I associate with them, it'll tear me down."

"I mean, I would be ignorant if I didn't hear some of the rumors in certain circles, Shelby. The Walkers aren't seen very well, for sure. It depends on what your family expects, I suppose. My parents know they aren't as welcomed in our circle and at the council, but they don't go out of their way to make their lives miserable. They are more passive."

"My parents aren't passive, that's for certain. But why do they have to go after Randy or Riley for what their parents did? And it's not like my parents are perfect. I just don't know what to do."

"You want to be their friends?"

"Yes."

"Then do that."

"What about my parents? Even my aunt has me considering their perspective."

"There won't be a perfect answer, Shelby. You'll have to make sacrifices one way or the other. You can attempt to be who you were with those friends going with whatever your parents ask of you, or you chart your own path and possibly defy your parents and deal with their repercussions. It comes down to what makes you happy."

I sighed. "This is hard."

Luke chuckled. "Yes, it can be. But I have a feeling you're the perfect person for that obstacle."

My throat emitted a strangled laugh. "I don't know about that. Like you said, I have an ooey-gooey center."

"That's true, but not in the way you're taking it. You have power from your family's legacy. You care about people; that's not a weakness, that's a strength."

"I didn't use to. Before Riley, I would have done what they said and relished in the perks and attention. I wasn't the … nicest."

"We all have those streaks. I'd be more surprised if you didn't. It doesn't matter who you *used to be*. It matters who you are now and what you're willing to do to maintain it."

"You're pretty wise, you know that?"

"I've been told once or twice."

I laughed. "Seriously. I feel so lost. I don't know what I'd do if I didn't have anyone to talk to about it."

"Well, you have me."

I smiled. "Thanks, Luke."

"Of course. I get it more than most."

I sighed. "Why do you have to be in boarding school?"

He chuckled. "Story of my life. But I'll be home at Easter break. And who knows, maybe I'll be able to get away over a long weekend."

"That'd be nice. Easter feels too far away." I watched the horizon as it darkened. I needed to return before it got too dark. "I guess I should go."

"Okay. Let me know what happens."

"Will do. Bye, Luke." I ended the call and shoved the phone in my coat pocket.

The walk back to the house was too quick. I wanted to linger and bask in the phone call. Luke was proving to be the best arranged date I'd had. He's become my friend, and right now that was more than I could have wished for.

~

Dinner had been extremely uncomfortable. We avoided any conversations without the use of a device. Most of the time, they weren't allowed, unless it was my father's, but I don't think we all had ever stared at our plates more than tonight. No one attempted to ease the tension, so when my mother left the table early, followed by my father, I had been more relieved than ever.

I asked chef Frank if I could take the meal upstairs, and, as soon as it was ready, I bolted with it from the kitchen.

My aunt hadn't appeared for dinner, but even if she had, I wasn't ready to talk to her yet either. She was on my list to talk to, but I had to figure out how to ignite her spark again. It wasn't right for her to seem so deflated. She was an exuberant person, not someone with so much self-doubt and defeat.

I scooted backward against my headboard and grabbed my phone. My threat to Tabitha and Priscilla earlier was for them to remove their post. Before now, I hadn't had the chance to check.

I clicked on the little bee icon on my phone and scrolled through the posts. Most at the top were about midterm updates, then halfway down, I found their post. The comments had exploded since I looked before.

Old news! Shelby has always been fake.

Of course, she's fake!

This really isn't a surprise, is it?

Randy and Riley are adorable. Leave them alone. As for Shelby, well, what do we expect from a Rowe?

I sighed. So many people really thought I was like that. I guess I couldn't blame them. When was the last time I had done something nice for my classmates? When had the Rowes done something nice? My father's company ran charities, but giving back to the *actual* people of the community was rare. It was always elite guests with invites, like at the Christmas ball.

Things needed to change; there was no more doubt.

I opened the group message with Tabitha and Priscilla.

Why is the post still up? Either take it down or be prepared for tomorrow. Don't mess with me.

I watched as three dots appeared at the bottom of our chat—someone was typing—then the dots disappeared.

I refreshed the app several times until, on the tenth time, the post disappeared. I smirked. They were still scared of me, and I could work with that.

$\mathcal{M}$y stomach flipped and cramped all morning as I waited for lunch. It was the best time to deal with what had happened the prior day. Riley, Randy, and Sophie would all be together and that would also make it easier to keep them together without them running away. If I didn't get to them soon, everything would go backward, and I absolutely didn't want to rebuild everything I had worked so hard on the past few weeks.

I peered into the cafeteria through the small windows in the doors. I wanted to see them before they saw me. If they saw me coming, I wouldn't have the opportunity to diffuse the situation. I needed them all to know I didn't do it. I hadn't said those things.

The trio sat at their table, heads bent in a deep conversation. Other people stared at them from surrounding tables. Tabitha and Priscilla weren't at our normal table.

It was either now or never.

The door swung open as I added a little pressure. I walked toward their table, lunchbox in hand, and only hoped they would listen.

If looks could kill, Sophie would have stopped me dead. Riley's face wasn't thrilled either, although less deadly. Randy's expression was unreadable.

I took a deep breath and sat.

Sophie glared. "I—"

"Before you yell, because I know it's coming, I wanted to tell you my side."

Sophie crossed her arms and muttered, "This'll be good."

Riley eyed me but stayed silent. I took it as a cue to continue.

"I didn't type those texts. I don't even use the word totally when I talk or type. And I know how I sound. I know this is like déjà vu, but I swear I'm not lying. I will let you go through all my texts if it helps prove I didn't do it. I value your friendships." I stared at each of them. "*All* of you. And I am so, so sorry Riley and Randy that you two were put on blast again. I wanted the opposite, and I will do whatever you want to rectify that."

"We've heard that before," Sophie huffed.

Riley eyed Sophie. "She's right. This has happened before. And even though I believe you haven't posted these statements in either case, your little henchmen, seem determined to make my life miserable. I just want to be left alone, and, if that's impossible to do as your friend, then I don't know if it's worth it."

"I understand. I do, but I really want to make this right. Tabitha and Priscilla removed it, and I don't plan to be friends with them again. I'm done. They've gone too far. I'll post about it on the Buzz app. I'll make a speech. I'd do whatever, because I want you to know I don't think that."

Sophie rolled her eyes.

I pleaded with Randy and Riley. Neither would really look at me. "I admire what you two are doing. You have a genuine connection, and you are taking it slow. I understand that. I think it's amazing. You ignore what others say about you two, and I wish I had that ability. I'll be the first to admit I was a lousy person last year and the years before that. I didn't realize what position I had and what I could do with it. I want to give others chances who didn't have the option before. And those two are answering to a higher up, which I fully plan to deal with too."

Randy sighed. "I don't care what was posted, Shelby. I know that's not who you are. But you must admit the drama escalated every time you try to be friends with us. Like Riley said, we just want to be left alone."

"So do I. Many of those comments were horrendous. They didn't even write about the text's content; it was about me. So many of our classmates think I'm fake."

Sophie snorted. "I wonder why. You avoid so many people you've gone to school with for years. You literally only talked to those two. No one asked you to be best friends with everyone, but you set the tone. You could have done something about it and never did. Until now." She crossed her arms. "Why should we believe you now? What has changed so much that you're different?"

"I know it's hard to believe. Riley started it, but I kept thinking about all the things I let happen in my life. How out of control it was. I get ripped in half on a daily basis. The expectations from my parents and the town. They all want me to be the Shelby Rowe they envision. I don't get to make a decision or choose. Do you know what that feels like to have your life decided by others?"

Sophie shook her head. Riley's head remained glued to the floor. Randy stroked Riley's hand as he focused on her face.

"Do you at least believe I didn't write those awful things?"

Riley shrugged. "You're showing more effort than last time, that's for sure. But how do we know this doesn't flip again in a few weeks? Or even with your input, they continue going after us."

"I don't think they will. Not like that. I have things on them too. I don't plan to use it, but they don't know that. If they say anything like that about you again, I'd unleash. Tabitha and Priscilla are scared. If they weren't, they wouldn't have removed it. They're floundering without me there. We were a team, just like you three are. At one point, I would have stuck up for them, but I don't like who they've become. Or who they act like now that I under-stand more."

Sophie huffed. "Fine. I'll agree to you staying here too. But I swear, Shelby, if you screw up again, you can forget it."

"I understand. You have my word."

Riley picked at her shirt. "Okay."

Yes! I was elated to get through to them. Now I had to get through to the others in my life.

～

"Aunt Delilah!" I screamed as I threw my books in my room and bounded down the hallway.

I had spent all day contemplating how I could talk to my aunt after I fixed things with Riley, Randy, and Sophie. They made me realize that no matter the choices we made in the past, we always have the time to do something different, and I think she needed that right now.

My aunt peered from the end of the hallway. "Is every-thing okay?"

"Oh, yeah. Sorry to scare you. I just wanted to make sure I caught you if you were home."

She leaned against the wall. "Oh? How come?"

"I wanted to let you know I talked to Riley and Randy. I think I'll have to put in some work to make them believe my innocence fully, but at least they listened to what I had to say this time."

"That's great, Shelby. What about your mother? Won't you be going against what she asked you?"

"That's what I wanted to talk to you about. Can I come in and sit down?"

"Sure."

I walked to the jade velvet-lined armed chair. I bounced a little on the cushion to get comfy and watched my aunt sit on another one opposite me. "I wanted to talk to you about yesterday. I don't know all the details of what happened with you, but I know this isn't you. You and I are kindred spirits. We've always gotten each other. So what, you dated a married man. Shame on him for not telling you he was married, and so what if you stayed a little longer after you knew. We can't help who we connect with, but I can't imagine something deflating you so completely that you would agree with my mother at any level. She might have a backstory that could make me sympathize, but it doesn't give her the authority to say things to you the way I know she has or act like she knows what's best in every situation."

"Maybe, but she's right about how much of a mess I've made."

I crossed my arms. "So, go fix it, then! You can't run from it; it won't change the reality of what happened. Figure out what you want to do and go from there, that's what I did."

"Lots of people witnessed the situation. It's not easy."

"Of course not. The situation with Randy and Riley is complicated too. So many moving parts and, honestly, going against my mother still kind of terrifies me in how she will retaliate, but I don't care. I need to do this for myself, and you need to fix it for you."

Delilah stood, arms outstretched. "Thank you, Shelby."

I embraced her. I hated to think that anything could crush her spirit so successfully.

She pulled away and looked into my eyes. "Do you have a plan for your mother?"

I shook my head. "I still need to find the best route."

"Just appeal to her agenda and you'll be fine."

My eyebrow rose. "How do I do that?"

"What does she always care about? Appearance, reputation."

I frowned. "How will I do that? She thinks my reputation and image is hindered from being their friends. You know, 'We are who we associate with.' It's her most used mantra."

"Make her believe your reputation will be better as friends."

"I don't know if it'll work. She's dead set in her ways, you know that."

"Well, your only other hope is to somehow outrank her."

"Outrank her?"

"Yeah. Get your father on board and she won't have a choice. She won't like it, but she'll listen if he says to leave it alone."

Hmm, was it possible to get him to be on my side? If anyone had the power to do it, he would. He might see things from a business standpoint easier, but it would take some persuading. Maybe at the next council meeting? If things went well, it was possible I could sway him.

I stroked my chin. "That just might work."

She squeezed my knee. "I hope so. And I'm sorry I didn't make you feel more supported at first."

"Don't worry about it. I heard what I needed to."

"I love you, Shelby."

"I love you too." I stood and winked at her.

I left her room and shuffled down the hallway to my room. The founders meeting could be the best place to win over my father, but was I ready? I secured my bedroom door and grabbed my phone. It took a minute to find Randy's number, and I opened our messages.

I have a plan for the founder's meeting. If we're successful, my father just may help with this whole situation and my mother interfering in who my friends are.

Randy replied quickly, *Sounds good. Let me know what I need to do.*

If this plan worked, my mother would no longer be a problem.

CHAPTER 24

The plan would work. It had to work.

I jiggled my leg as I waited for the council meeting to start. This was a big meeting. Companies had to bring their notes on best sellers and any other services they could provide for a festival. Randy had agreed to let me take point on the presentation. If I could sweeten up my dad, then our conversation afterward could work. It *had* to work.

I made eye contact with Randy.

He gave me two thumbs up, but it did nothing for my nerves. If today didn't go well, I'd have to wait too long before I could use another council meeting to try again.

My father breezed into the room and sat next to me.

The other members quieted and looked to him to begin.

"Good morning, gentlemen and Shelby. It's time we begin today's meeting. Let us start with the work on the festivals. If you could all pass the data to Shelby to peruse while we deal with some of the other agenda points, that would be great. Then, at the end, we will discuss some pointers."

I waited as the packets came toward me. Randy and I had agreed to let me handle the packets. We could talk later to find out what he wanted to do too, but this time, it was all mine. Good or bad, it would be my fault, my ideas. I scanned the first packet as I drowned out the rest of the meeting. They discussed something about town updates and new projects, but I needed to focus. It would be my turn before I realized, and I wanted to be prepared.

Focus, Shelby!

The first packet was from Mr. Tate. His company was less involved with the bees. They worked more with the farming industries, providing and maintaining equipment for the farms. How would we use his top tractors? Could we use them for transportation? To pull a wagon? There were hayrides in the fall, but could we do something similar in the spring? Maybe with flowers? Pamphlets could showcase the equipment for other nearby farms.

I made a few notes on my legal pad and moved to the next packet that contained products like lip balm, lotions, and other makeup options. This would work perfectly for the booth idea Randy and I had contemplated.

The next few packets were similar. We would have to locate them around the area to give them equal opportunities with customers.

The final packet was more about services, marketing specifically. That could work for promoting the festival and other products. Then there was Randy's products from his family and ours from Rowe Industries. We didn't need to promote our products; if anything, I hoped to convince my father to donate some.

We could also hold a silent auction with the products for companies willing to donate. My only hope was they would go for it. I jotted down a few more notes and kept a close eye on the meeting. I still had time; they seemed to have taken a detour when it came to some of the maintenance projects in town. I hadn't listened close enough to know why it would take them so long, but I would take it. Any extra time meant well-prepared ideas to present to the council.

I drew a rough sketch of the town center; the perfect place for the festival would be closer to the park, but some of the restaurants and other businesses near the festival should be involved. We could have Over Easy's prepare food closer to the festival or make it a scavenger hunt.

Yes! That's it!

We should do a scavenger hunt of the best places to visit in town. Families who visited them all within the duration of the festival and weeks before and after could earn a prize or complimentary goods. It would be perfect to involve some of the other community businesses in town.

I finished scrawling my notes on my legal pad as my father turned his chair to me.

He leaned over and whispered, "Are you ready to present?"

I nodded.

"Good. We're almost ready." My father cleared his throat and stood, buttoning his jacket as he went. "Gentleman, I think we can table this discussion for now, don't you?"

Many averted their gazes, clearly not ready to move on. But what my father wanted, my father got.

"Good. We're ready for my daughter, Shelby, to present her ideas on a step forward in this festival."

I stood and glanced at my father.

Before I could speak, Mr. Tate raised his hand near my face. "Wait a minute. Why are we listening to *your* daughter, Thaddeus? She may be a Rowe, but what does she know? I don't think you've proven to us that she is knowledgeable in this subject."

My father's eyes narrowed. He geared up for an argument; I could see it in his stance. He sat like he was ready to pounce.

Instead, I laid my hand on his shoulder and patted. I met his gaze and hoped my eyes said, *I'll handle it*. I needed a chance to show I knew what I was doing and that I could do it myself.

"Mr. Tate, I completely understand your concerns. I'm a female in high school, and I don't attend all the meetings this fine council has. What would I know?" I paused to allow Mr. Tate to nod and look superior—give him a false sense of security and then strike. "I assure you, as Homecoming Queen, a member of student council, and the daughter of Vivian Rowe who has successfully planned and coordinated a Christmas ball for fifteen years, as well as the daughter of Thaddeus Rowe, owner and CEO of Rowe Industries, I am the right person for this job. I have been attending and watching the planning of many successful events in my lifetime. As someone with such experience, I understand what to look for and where to start."

"I-I ..." Mr. Tate said.

"I'll take that as your approval." I regarded my father and the other members of the council, all who appeared to be happy with my explanation. "Now, I have perused your packets as much as possible, and I see several themes. First, we have many companies with products to market. I suggest we utilize this in several ways—incorporate booths in a marketlike style around the park for visitors to peruse as they enjoy the festivities. Second, I suggest doing a silent auction based on a theme and using donated products to create those baskets. It will get exposure, and the money for the baskets would have a percent that remained with the company, and the rest would help cover costs for the festival. Finally, I believe, for the month of the festival, there should be a scavenger hunt with local businesses. The businesses in town should decorate according to the theme of the festival, but then, as patrons visit those places, their cards are hole punched. If they make it to all the establishments, they receive some sort of incentive."

The men mumbled and stroked their chins.

"I like it!" Mr. Walker announced.

"Yes, well, that's great for those with products. What about us with tractors? I can't gift one in a basket," Mr. Tate said.

"Yes, well, you aren't alone, Mr. Tate. For our companies that have services, like marketing, they will help create the cards for the scavenger hunts, posters for the festival, and run online campaigns that our companies send out. Mr. Tate, your tractors can be set up and used for something like a springtime-themed hayride."

"Hmm, that could work," Mr. Tate said.

I looked to my father whose expression was a suppressed grin.

His eyes crinkled in the corner, and he kept his hands still.

As far as I could tell, my plan was working.

"Let's take a vote on these ideas," my father said. "All in favor, raise your hands."

I scanned the room, and without hesitation, all the hands rose within a matter of seconds.

"Okay, then we have a direction. We will contact each company before next council's meeting to set up what items they're donating and about booking a table at the festival."

I sat and beamed. This was my chance. Things had gone better than I had expected. If I couldn't win my father over today, I never would.

He squeezed my knee as he continued the meeting. I heard nothing of what he said, but I focused on the feeling. I had to play it right, or it would all go to waste.

～

e scooted into the vehicle and waited as the driver closed our door and started the car.

"That was brilliant today, Shelby. I knew you always had it in you."

I smiled. "Thanks. I told you I could do it."

"Yes, you did."

"See, I listen to you and Mother. I focus on your skills and your abilities."

"Well, I'll agree with that. You won them all over, even Tate. What a smug buffoon."

I giggled. "He definitely doesn't like me much."

My father waved me off. "He doesn't know what he's talking about. He just likes to throw a wrench in everything I do."

"His niece is no different."

"Well, you shut him up fast. I thought it would go down-hill from there, but you recovered very nicely."

"Thank you." I fiddled with my coat. I wouldn't get another time to ask. I just hoped it worked. "I was wondering if I could talk to you about something."

He peered from his phone. "What's that?" He shoved the phone in his pocket.

Always a good sign.

I took a deep breath. "I wanted to talk about Riley and Randy again. Now before you say anything, I want you to hear me out. Randy and I worked successfully today. Yes, I looked at the packets, and I made decisions, but they were based off our discussions previously. I know you worry about the Walker family, but what if his son is different than Silas? They weren't always on the outside of the council. The hit on the bee populations affected everyone. If we hadn't had more capital than they did, we could have faced similar consequences." I scanned his face—completely neutral, which was better than pure rage. "We are who we associate with, but what if we are looking at it all wrong? Our family could be admired if we start *helping* other companies. When was the last time we truly did something selfless? And before you object, think about the growth opportunities from that. Something happened at school the other day, and many people see Rowes as ruthless, cutthroat people. How can they trust us? Engage with our company if they don't feel reciprocity with it?"

My father stroked his chin, seeming to contemplate what I had said.

"I'm proposing we use a probationary period. I get to hang out with Randy and Riley without mother's interference in school, so long as I maintain my duties and show that a true friendship will go a long way for our brand and reputation. We want the community to be able to count on us. Only then will they continue to promote us and use our products. It's not just having top quality, it's also who we are as a company, which is based on the Rowe name. We must consider the climate of today's world. Ignoring subsets of the population would be detrimental to our success."

He raised his hand to silence me. "I can tell you have put a lot of thought into this, Shelby. I'm willing to accept your proposal. I agree that times have changed, and we must ensure Rowe Industries aren't looked at as greedy people. You're right that employees and consumers want to feel cared about in order for production to increase. You have a deal. There will be no interference, but, if you slip on your duties or social obligations, it will end."

"You mean it?"

He nodded.

I beamed. It was a win, and I would take it. My mother wouldn't be happy, but she wouldn't oppose my father. It wouldn't suit her as a proper wife.

"Can I ask one more thing?"

He cocked his eyebrow. "More?"

"Not about them. I was wondering about you and Mother. You've been gone a lot lately, and things have been tense. Are you two okay?"

His face softened. "Of course, Shelby. I've been busy solidifying new business deals. Your mother understands, even if she doesn't always like my being away so much."

"So, you two aren't fighting? Or separating?"

He squeezed my hand. "No. We're okay. Things are slowing down a little more, and I'll be home until the summer. You know how the busy season goes."

"It seemed like more than the busy season. You've never left so often during Christmas time. Are you … Are you avoiding us?"

His eyes widened. "What? No. Is that what you thought?"

"Mother has been upset more, and you've been gone a lot this December."

He sighed. "Things with Rowe Industries are good, all things considered, but we did take hits to our revenue when the mites invaded the town. We don't have to downsize or anything, like some companies are, but we haven't escaped unscathed. I've been meeting with outside companies to invest more money in the company. I want to ensure this didn't cause more setbacks. Year's end is the best time to solicit companies' leftover money, because they don't have to pay taxes on it."

Was that really the issue? He really had been on business trips?

"It's a tricky deal though, because some companies are tapped out in December. It took more face-to-face meetings to get the deals done."

"So, you don't have another family somewhere to replace us?"

"No, absolutely not, Shelby. Your mother and I might not be the most tender couple, but I'm not out looking for another family. Your mother doesn't deal with the business, so she doesn't know why I was so busy."

My eyebrow arched. "Why wouldn't you tell her?"

"That's not our arrangement."

"But, if I could think it, couldn't she?"

He scratched his forehead and paused. "I don't think so, but I'll be home more now that the new year has started. We have the funds we had searched for, so now business can be completed from conference calls."

"You're sure?"

"Yes."

"Well, I'm glad you two are okay. We miss you when you're gone."

He smiled. "I miss you too."

I squirmed in my seat. "Mother will be upset about this deal with Randy and Riley."

He shrugged. "I'll explain to her how it's best for our family. Don't worry. I'll tell her with you."

I nodded. One down, one more to go. And then maybe, just maybe, my life would be in *my* control for once.

CHAPTER 25

My smiled shattered the second I crossed the threshold. My mother wouldn't take this conversation well, even though I ultimately knew she would listen to my father. Expecting no repercussions though was stupid. She would find a way to get back at me, albeit not about Riley and Randy. Would it be more chores? More responsibilities? I didn't know for certain, but I knew it would be something.

I waited for my father to enter. We would talk to my mother together.

The clacking sound echoed through the foyer. She stopped and stared at me.

"Hello, Mother."

She crossed her arms and stayed silent, eyeing me warily.

We hadn't talked in a while; did she think I was already scheming something? I fiddled with my coat. What was taking my father so long to get inside?

Finally, he opened the door and strolled inside. "Vivian, perfect timing. I need to discuss something with you."

"Oh?"

He handed his belongings to Mr. Bennet. "You're to let Shelby be friends with Randy and Riley. She must maintain her responsibilities, but no more interfering."

Mother's jaw slackened, and her gaze narrowed. "Excuse me?"

I cleared my throat. This wasn't good at all.

"She had a wonderful presentation today at the council meeting. She opened my eyes to how the community perceives our reputation. If we expect to grow, we need to keep in mind what the town thinks of us."

"Precisely, which is why being around those two isn't a good idea."

"Actually, Mother, that's not true. If we can show the community that we care about families like the Walkers— even *rehabilitate* them—then the community would be more invested in us and therefore the company. If they think we're greedy, why would they support us?"

"Who says we're greedy? No one thinks that. Just look at our attendance at the Christmas ball."

I narrowed my gaze. "You mean of the elite families in town? You won't even let me visit certain establishments because they are *below* us. What message are we sending them?"

She crossed her arms. "Thaddeus, you can't be serious. She doesn't know what she's talking about."

My father scrunched his nose at her. "How doesn't she? She did well with the council today. Do you know how hard it is to impress them? Even Mr. Tate agreed with her plans. *She* did that. *You* didn't. So, until I see that she isn't furthering this family, then why can't she choose her friends? Your method isn't working."

My mother tapped her foot. "This is absurd. She'll ruin her reputation!"

"No, Mother. You're afraid I'd ruin *yours*. You act like

we're royalty, like we're the most important family in this town. We aren't. The town succeeds and fails together. And, if those families believe we don't care, what happens when the younger generation doesn't want to invest in our company? It won't exist. We can't treat people like trash and expect them to come back. Your little stunt with Tabitha and Priscilla made people talk. They think I'm fake. That Rowes are fake. If we don't fix it—it doesn't matter how many balls you've had—we'll be no better than the families you deem unworthy."

My father looked at me. "Remember your tone, Shelby. She's still your mother." He refocused on my mother. "Vivian, just give it a try. Shelby is perceptive. We've raised her under our wings. Don't you think she's learned things from us? Don't you trust her to keep us in mind?"

Mother crossed her arms and scowled. "I suppose I have no other choice."

My father smiled. "Thank you, dear. I knew you'd understand."

"I'm going to work on homework. Catch you both for dinner," I said as I bolted from the room. If my father left before my mother did, I knew I would hear about it more. I just needed her to have a little time to calm down and ruminate about the idea.

I ran past my room and skipped to my aunt's bedroom door. I knocked and let myself in. "Aunt Delilah!"

"I'll be right out!" she shouted from the bathroom.

I plopped in the chair and beamed. I had won. I could be friends with Riley and Randy, and maybe even Sophie—if she let me.

Aunt Delilah emerged from the bathroom. "What's up, Shelby?"

"I have good news!"

Her eyebrows rose. "About?"

"I convinced my father to let me be friends with Riley and Randy, which means he convinced my mother to do the same!"

"That's great." Delilah giggled. "I'm sure your mother was cross."

"Of course, she was, but it's the perfect plan. She won't go against my father, and who knows maybe eventually she'll be okay with it."

Delilah wrinkled her nose. "I doubt she'll ever be okay with it, but at least she won't interfere. That alone is a success."

"This is true. She's stubborn."

Delilah laughed. "Yes, she is. But we all are in this family. You get it naturally."

"Any progress for you?"

"I've decided I'll go back to my apartment and find a new job. It won't be easy, but I can't run from it anymore. If you can stand up to your mother, I can stand up to the stares."

I embraced her. "I think that's a great plan. But I'll miss you."

"I'll miss you too. But I promise to come visit you more often. I've got to see how your budding romance is going."

I cocked my eyebrow. "My budding *what?*"

"Don't play coy with me. I know you've shifted your feelings for Luke."

I crossed my arms. "I did not."

"Did too. It's okay if you like him, Shelby. It's okay to trust other people. Most people don't sabotage relationships like you're used to. It's time you trust in others and know that, for the most part, they'll stay by your side. Grow that group of people. Life is better that way."

I smiled. "Well, in that case, I have a plan I need you to help me with."

"Oh?"

I walked toward the door. "It starts in the kitchen. You coming?"

She trailed behind me. There was only one other thing to do to celebrate my win against my mother and the beginning of new friends. I had to bake.

~

I shuffled the batch of my famous red velvet cupcakes to the other hand as I crawled from Delilah's rental. I surveyed the perfect wraparound porch as I waited for Aunt Delilah to exit the car too.

After I had convinced her to help me bake cupcakes, I had informed her that we then had to deliver them.

"Whose house is this?" she asked.

"Our pinochle friend's house—Penny Brooks. Her granddaughter Riley lives with her, and I thought it would be fitting to shove our faces with sugar and maybe play some cards."

"Ah, that's why you made me bring the decks?"

I giggled. "Yep, just in case."

I knocked on the front door and scooted backward to wait for someone to answer. Riley's Impala sat in the driveway, so I knew she was home. I just didn't know if they were busy.

A smiling face answered the door. "Shelby! What a surprise!" Penny said in her southern drawl.

"I thought maybe we could all indulge on some sugar and play cards?"

Penny's eyes widened. "Sugar?"

"My famous red velvet cupcakes. All homemade."

Penny propped open the door with her elbow and leaned forward to help carry the cupcakes. "Mmm. Come in!"

I smiled as I walked through the doorway then stopped in

the grand hallway. "I was wondering if I could talk to Riley for a minute or so before?"

"Of course, darlin'. I'll put these on a plate in the kitchen. Delilah, right?"

My aunt nodded.

"Want to come help me?"

"Sure."

I smiled, thankful she had taken the cue that I wanted to talk to Riley alone.

Penny peered up the stairs and shouted, "Riley you have a visitor."

Shuffling feet echoed from upstairs until a door creaked open. Riley peered from the top of the stairs and scrunched her face when she saw me. She hopped down the stairs. "Shelby? What are you doing here?"

"I wanted to let you know what happened. *Everything* that happened. I think it's important you know the whole truth if we're going to be friends."

Riley gulped loudly.

"I learned recently, during a fight, that my mother is the cause of those details getting to Tabitha and Priscilla. She influenced them in some way to write that post in the fall because I had been too close to you. She has this annoying saying that we are who we associate with. I didn't know at the time, and like I've said, I felt so horrible they wrote those things." I watched Riley's eyes to gauge her expression, but it was emotionless."I asked her if you could go to the ball, and she said no, even though I didn't know Randy had already invited you. She thought it was somehow my doing, and then when I worked with Randy for a council meeting, my parents lost their minds. They told me I needed to ditch you all and stay away. But I didn't agree, so I didn't listen. Then you saw, once again, my mother retaliate. But I have good news."

Riley's eyes widened. "There's good news after all of that?"

"Yes. I made a deal with her and my father. They will leave you both alone if I maintain my duties as a Rowe. I'm allowed to be your friends, and they won't interfere again. My mother promised. And more importantly, my father will make sure she abides. So, no more random posts throwing you or me under the bus. I have no control over Tabitha and Priscilla—not really, anyway—but I don't suspect they would do anything on their own."

"I see." She sat at the bottom stair. "That's a lot. Wow. Sorry, I'm trying to process all of this."

"I understand it seems less worth it with all the drama that has happened, but I can assure you it won't happen again from my parents. And I really do think we could be friends if we gave it a try without all the interference."

Riley tucked a strand of hair behind her ears. "I can tell you're sincere about all of this, so I'm okay with trying, as long as this Shelby sticks around." She elbowed me lightly.

I smiled. "Absolutely. I brought my velvet cupcakes."

"You did? Oh, those things are delicious."

"Thank you. I thought maybe we could play cards? My aunt came with me. It could be fun."

Riley smiled. "I like that, even though I have no idea how to play."

"No problem. I'm rusty, and you're a shoe in. Your mom-mom is fabulous at pinochle."

"Then let's go shuffle those cards!"

I chuckled. "Sounds good."

I lagged behind Riley as I removed my phone. I had promised to let Luke know how the plan with my dad went. I opened our messages and texted. *I did it! I wowed the council with my ideas based on their data. I even shut down Mr. Tate and won over my father. He was in such a good mood that I convinced him to let go of the baggage with Riley and Randy's families. He told my mother the same thing and now I'm home free!*

I looked up and followed the sound of voices to the kitchen.

My aunt and Penny were laughing as Riley watched, taking a bite of her cupcake.

I didn't expect to ever have the chance to have real friends. I never expected that, at the beginning of this school year, I would have wanted a life different from my own.

My phone chirped. *I knew you could do it, Shelby! I know that had to be hard, but that's great.*

I smiled and watched. I soaked up every second of this moment, because, for once, every choice I made was my own, and it felt amazing.

"You ready to play?" Riley asked.

"Absolutely."

I stowed my phone and focused on the people who surrounded me in that moment. I felt more love than I had in years, and maybe, just maybe, this time I could get the ending I wanted for a change.

The Spring Renews
Book 3 in the Honey Cove Series
Coming May 2021

ACKNOWLEDGMENTS

This book would not have been possible without the help of many people. First, I want to thank my publisher Creative James Media for continuing to believe in my ideas.

I also want to thank Brian Paone for his wonderful editing services. Diana TC for her amazing cover work.

Alaine Greyson is my critique partner without whom I would be lost. She never tires of reading my drafts, no matter how many times she has seen it.

To my beta readers: KOBM, DM, and Johanna. You all helped me immensely to make this book the way it is. I am grateful for the feedback and time you spent on this story.

Finally to my family for dealing with my craziness towards deadlines and encouraging me to take risks and follow my dreams.

Please consider leaving a review after reading.
Goodreads Review
Amazon Review

For the latest news and updates, please check out Marie McGrath on her social media pages. Exclusive content and sneak peeks can be found in her FB Fan Page.

Twitter: @Marie_McGrath_
Instagram: marie_mcgrath_
Facebook: www.facebook.com/MarieMcGrathAuthor
Facebook Fan Page: www.facebook.com/groups/MarieMcGrathFans
Website: https://mariemcgrathauthor.wixsite.com/books
Newsletter: https://mailchi.mp/a07cddcef872/marie-mcgrath-fans

ABOUT THE AUTHOR

Marie McGrath lives in a small rural town in Maryland. She hopes to inspire others with her stories. Her favorite genres to read are YA Romance and Contemporary Fiction. She loves the color turquoise, lions, and listening to music.

www.ingramcontent.com/pod-product-compliance
Lightning Source LLC
Chambersburg PA
CBHW021124110726
47900CB00007B/2325